THE REAL JAZZ BABY

THE REAL JAZZ BABY

REFLEX FICTION VOLUME TWO

REFLEX PRESS

First published as an anthology in 2019 by Reflex Press
Abingdon, Oxfordshire, OX14 3SY
www.reflex.press

A CIP catalogue record of this book is available
from the British Library.

ISBN: 978-1-9161115-2-3

1

Printed and bound in Great Britain by
Clays Ltd, Elcograf S.p.A.

www.reflex.press/the-real-jazz-baby/

FOREWORD

When we launched Reflex fiction in December 2016, one of our main objectives was to showcase the versatility of flash fiction by publishing stories from a wide range of authors. How are we doing? At the time of going to press, we've published over 800 flash fictions by 550 different authors, each demonstrating a unique approach to the form. It is only through the generosity of those authors who allow us to publish their stories on our website, even when they've missed out on a prize, that we've been able to achieve our objective.

Inside these pages you'll find 162 stories from over 120 of the best flash fiction writers in the world, all long-listed for the four rounds of the Reflex flash fiction competition held in 2018. You'll find four winning stories: 'The Endless Conversation With My Mother' by E L Norry; 'Crowbar' by Lyndsay Wheble; 'My Father Comforts Me in the Form of Birds' by Sharon Telfer; and the story that gives this anthology its name, 'The Real Jazz Baby' by Fiona J Mackintosh.

The Real Jazz Baby is the perfect introduction to readers new to flash fiction, and essential reading for those already familiar with what the form can offer.

We would like to thank our guest judges Michelle Elvy, Sherrie Flick, Annemarie Neary, and David Swann, and our team of volunteer readers coordinated by Katy Hill.

David Borrowdale
Editor
Reflex Press

My Father Comforts Me in the Form of Birds
Sharon Telfer
SPRING 2018 FIRST PLACE

Heron
The December tarmac's glazing treacherous black. My mind should be on the road, not with my mother, left in the echoing house.

I take the roundabout too fast.

There it is, standing guard. I've never seen one here. No water, only frozen fields. Sentinel grey, crunched into its awkward bones, those quilling eyebrows. Unmistakable.

I hear his voice.

'Hamba gashle.'

'What's that, Dad?'

'It's Zulu. It means...'

I whisper it back as the light fades.

'...Go safely.'

I flip the visor against the falling sun.

Pheasant
We startle them into clattering flight. Survivors, seeing the New Year in against the odds.

One stays grounded, escorts us like a maverick sheepdog hitching a walk.

That look. *'Dad?'* Joking.

It stops. Its feathers glint rainbows in the iced light.

That sideways look. *'Is that you, Dad?'* Half-joking.

The absurd lens of grief.

Sparrowhawk?
Hard to tell. We pass so quickly.

Roadside perch. Sharp eyes scanning.

'What do I always say?'

'Keep your options open, Dad.'

Robin
On a clear day, you can see the hills he loved from here.

This is not a clear day.
Every voice feels winter-stopped.
In the branches, a spot of red, defiant.
'The robin keeps singing right through the winter.'
Its sweet strain clarifies the clouded air.
'Very few birds do that, you know.'
The mist begins to lift, a little.

Goldfinch

The feeders have swung empty for months. We knock the nails in lower so Mum can reach, refill them with rich sunflower hearts.

'They're back!'

From the kitchen window, we watch a charm of gold glitter the garden.

Curlew

Spring loops in on that cool, clear call, back to breed on the hard, high moors.

'That day we found a nest, remember? The baby curlew? The parent bird circling overhead?'

The wind lifts heady scent from the greening woods, scatters blossom like confetti, accepts the ash we offer.

Skylark

You hear it first, notes like diamonds etching glass.

Lift your head. Turn your face to the full sun.

'Look long enough, you will see it.'

There, infinitesimal in the infinite blue.

Do you see him?

Yes! There! Rising, singing, rising...

The Shape of Us

Christopher M Drew

SPRING 2018 SECOND PLACE

We lie on a bed of meadow-grass. Long stems surround us, arching their backs against the wind.

You strike a match and cup your hand around the flame. The cigarette tip glows like a dying star, burning substances into nonexistence.

Above us, two airplanes curve through the sky toward each other. Our hands join as they collide, two bodies connected not by gravity, or magnetism, or fate, but by something else, something immeasurable, a resonance of energy between them.

I imagine the aircraft falling in pieces around us, but after a moment they separate, thousands of feet apart. As you turn to gather your clothes, I trace my lips over the pattern of grass that covers your skin like a scar.

We stand and dress, slipping into our mud-stained trousers, our creased shirts.

You smile and straighten my collar. Behind you, the sun rises.

A narrow track winds through the trees and out onto the road. We follow the path side by side, our shoulders touching and separating again and again.

It's the Casimir effect, you say. Two objects this close together will always attract one another.

I don't tell you that I dream of the entire universe, all that emptiness expanding, everything moving away from everything else.

You climb into your station wagon and start the engine. Dust kicks up from the tyres, a wall between us.

Walking back along the trail, I wait at the meadow's edge to watch the flattened grass stalks reach out toward the sun, the shape of us softening as gently as a kiss, our memory fading like contrails in the distance.

Uffizi

Conor Montague

SPRING 2018 THIRD PLACE

We stand looking at David, him starkers as the day he was born.
I'm disappointed in the size of his penis. I mean it's flaccid and all
but even so, after the way you built him up... I turn to you, say
nothing. Look back to David's crotch, curve of your hip snug in
my palm, peach blossom fragrant from frizzed hair. A scruff
mooches to our side, smug beneath ragged cream fedora. He too
seems unimpressed, tilts head, scratches earlobe. You poke my
ribs.

'What do you think?'

Penis shatters, balls drop, flat crack pulses through *Piazza*.
Another crack: and another. Your chest spews scarlet mist. Clasp
you as you slump, swirl from stoneless David. A man-child pans
a Kalashnikov. Pilgrims scuttle over cobblestones, dive into arch-
ways, drop to join bloodied lumps strewn across the square like
one of those Tate Modern installations you drag me to. Mottled
fedora flitters through grey gritted air.

Man-child explodes, a brief Goliath. Plinth shatters spine. I'm
blind, broken, sound a raging ringing torrent, peach blossom fragrant through dust of bitter centuries. Flash to you in Boboli Gar-
dens this morning, eyes ablaze as you coaxed a blooming sapling
to you and inhaled the world.

Inside, a Stone
Christopher M Drew

Our eyes meet across the crowded bar, and in this moment, before you pay for your drink, before you zip your purse, before you smile and turn away, we know everything about each other. I know that you spend most of your weekends at home and will never set foot in this dive again. You know that I come here every night and sit on the same stool until closing. I know that you hate places like this, that you don't drink, that the whole damn office came out and you couldn't think of an excuse fast enough. You know that I am alone, that I have been alone for a long time. I know that you're tired, and angry, and afraid. That you wish you were somebody else. You know that I feel the same. The only difference is that I have already lost who I am, and you are still searching. I know that I could love you. If only I had the courage to grab my coat, walk over to you, and say *Hello*. But you know that if I do this, it would destroy you. We share this moment, when our eyes meet, and everything that we have been and are and could be stretches out forever, as beautiful and devastating as a supernova. I see light bursting from our centre. You see it too, but you've seen it before, and you know the truth. You know that, in time, fire turns to ash, ash to smoke, smoke to dust. That in the heart of a supernova is a cold, hard stone. In this moment, we are everything we're supposed to be, and nothing could be more perfect than this.

I grab my coat.

A Little Something I'll Never Send
Alicia Bakewell

You cried into your pillow, then my shoulder, then your pillow again. I wished you would shut up. Don't get me wrong, I hated myself for that. I'm not a total monster. While you slept, having exhausted yourself, I envied your peace of mind. I stayed the night, feeling I had no choice.

You wanted to talk, to reminisce, only I'd never met your brother. All I could do was comfort you. As I rubbed your back, my thoughts drifted to the other bad news, the thing I couldn't tell you. Not now. I felt the letter's sharp corners in my pocket. I'd give it to you in the morning, maybe.

Your mother was coming from Dublin for the funeral. Finally, reluctantly, I would meet her. How could I say no in the circumstances? Her favourite colour was purple, you told me, so perhaps I could wear it. Come on, you knew me well enough by then. I'd be wearing black, and not just because it was a funeral.

So I couldn't give you the letter while your mother was there, could I? She was nice, by the way, nothing like I was expecting. I ate underfilled jam tarts, drank warm filter coffee and smiled at your relatives for both of us when you couldn't. We rode home in the funeral company car, and your Ma complimented my hair, but not my dress.

Grief changed you in small ways. The long silences gave you a bit of Zen. You would dream of him sometimes and reach for my hand in the dark. Your eyes grew soulful, watered and nourished by all those tears. And when you ran out of stories to tell about your brother, we would just sit and talk about anything and everything. Your voice had become quieter, and it suited you.

I've still got the letter. It's from the old me, written to the old you. Parts of it are still true. We've got nothing in common. You have no ambition. Your sense of humour is a little odd, and that's me being kind. But the bit about not loving you? Well, I've reconsidered.

Beneath Sakura
Adam Lock

The branches grow from her left hip like lightening moving up and across her back. Cherry blossom, each flower dusk-pink, grey-veined. The Japanese call it Sakura. Her body is all turns: curving shoulder blades, bending spine, buckling ribcage. But I don't know if the tattoo means she loves her body or hates it.

From the left, a speedboat tears a white line between sea and sky. If I rest my eyes, focus as far out to sea as I can, the horizon bends to the curvature of the earth and the sky is a dome.

She stands, her back to me, arranges her white bikini briefs. She's young. I don't remember ever going topless on a beach. Years ago, I had skin like hers, same arms, same legs.

'Why would she do that?' Martin says, kicking sand as he leans over, breathless, offering one of the drinks in his hands. 'Pretty thing like that, and she does that to her skin.'

'I think it's beautiful.'

'You would,' he says, sitting on the sun-bed next to mine.

The woman reaches to the back of her head, ties her dark hair into a tidy bundle. Her skin shines with oil. The branches on her skin, the open pink flowers, the closed white buds, sway back and forth as she moves.

In Japan, if the weather is kind, cherry blossom can last a week. But there are some years, if the wind is fierce, if the rain falls hard, it can disappear in hours, even minutes. Every year the Japanese picnic beneath blooming Sakura.

I reach behind to unfasten my bikini top. Martin watches, mouth open. I drop my bikini top onto the sand between our sun-beds.

In the next life, I'll picnic beneath Sakura like the Japanese.

Cutting the Thread
Lee Hamblin

My grandmother was born into a world of truths in a place not here. She talks about her gods without fear of ridicule because she knows the comfort of faith. She is old, and we know that she will die soon, and when I go to her room and hold her hand, her smile brings me a tear of beautiful sad. On her bedside table are three things: a glass of water rarely sipped, a candle always lit, and a blackwood frame with three oval windows, each window cherishing a photograph shrouded by the candle's ring of light.

She is young in the first portrait, about my age now. I tell her she looks like the sun. Where have you been lately? she asks. Oh, you know, I reply, busy at college. She smiles. It's true; she does look like the sun in the first photograph, the morning sun, the one that waltzes into every day no matter what. The sun makes me happy, I tell her; it gives me life. *Brahman*, she says, is the giver of life. Maybe they're one and the same I think but decide to keep the thought to myself.

In the second photograph, she resembles my mother—her daughter. But unlike my mother, the pomegranate-red lipstick she wears is not a wish for yesteryear. The flesh furrows around her eyes, sags beneath her jaw. But I see everything in her eyes: stifling summers, biting winters, winds strong enough to topple the strongest tree, pelting rains that flood yet nourish. And still her eyes smile love at me.

The third portrait is her not long after she arrived here. The skin of her cheeks is now cracked, and her eyes tinge sorrow, or disbelief, or wonder; it's hard to say. You look scared in this one, I tell her. For you, yes, she replies. For you.

She sits up, adjusts her pillow, asks for a little water. I guide the glass to her lips. She cradles my hand in hers. Now, my *jaan*, she says, go get your mother, *Shiva* is coming. And when I look at her, she's shining like the sun once again.

How to Bake an Earthquake
Leonora Desar

I am collecting men. The first is a chef. He smells like roses and mulled wine. He smells like voodoo candles and this sweet city, and sometimes I curl up in his beard and sleep. Your walls are so blank and white, he says. They are so hungry, he says, I can hear them growling when I push my ear against them. That's just the pipes, I say. These walls need feeding, he says. The chef is like an ad for my husband's shaving cream—*Clean. Close. Comfortable.* My husband is like the French version—*Rasage Net. De près. Et Confortable.* He says he's comfortable but how can he be with all those French vowels sticking in his mouth? My husband likes the walls the way they are. I think those walls need feeding, I say. The chef takes out a marker. A pen. *Three scoops nutmeg. Two tablespoons cinnamon. Add pecan. And don't forget: 10 cups cayenne pepper.* The words curl up like ivy on the plaster. My nana's recipe for cinnamon pecan pie, he says, looking very pleased. He's such a big man, not the type to have a nana, off cooking somewhere in some little room, an attic, maybe, or a Victorian house down by the sea. To have words that look like a lost little boy in the big white infinite of my husband's basement. Something about this pie seems fishy, but I don't want to disappoint him, not the way he's looking at me, and kissing me, and now the walls are sighing, they're purring, like a hamster in a soft, dark palm. For the rest of the day, I feel tingly, spicy. When the chef's not looking I spoon the walls and lick.

Shattered
Gillian Rioja

I observe a shoal of silver fish then roll on my back and bob with the swell. In the white, hazy sky a plane drifts in front of the sweltering Arab sun. Which of the three countries that border this bay is it heading for? The guidebook says western swimwear is acceptable, but I feel more respectful in T-shirt and shorts, although my stomach presses against the waistband.

There's Paul on the shore, finishing his hummus sandwich. A rather scruffy beach, we agreed, with cigarette butts half-buried in the sand and rubbish caught on thorn-bushes, but peaceful and convivial. Near Paul, that noisy family is preparing an elaborate meal, their picnic table covered with bowls of salad and rice. Shouts, cries, laughter; the universal language of children at play. I stroke my tummy, in just seven months...

A woman in a golden headscarf sits in the shallow waters; her gown, an aquatic flower, floats around her. Burkini-clad girls hold each other's hands and, like playful seals, rise and fall with the waves. They see me looking over and smile. A toddler, held by his father at arm's length, bounces up and down. For a second the man lets go. The child gives a delighted squeal, his podgy arms reach out and he grasps the father, a limpet to a pier. Who feels more loved, the protector or the protected?

A boom like far-away thunder. Confusion on the father's face, the toddler howls. Why is Paul standing, the children silent, everyone staring at the sky? Look up. Billow of black smoke shot through with flames. Debris dropping into the distant sea. Is that a propeller?

Paul is running towards me. Behind him, black plastic bags tug on the thorns like tethered ravens trying to break free.

Message Received
Dawn Thompson

The foetus knows. Its cells sense danger. Father intervenes. Disallows the friend's whispered advice. Stops the frantic floor-scrubbing. Runs cold into the too-hot bathwater. Tosses the bottle of laxatives. 'It' becomes I, still embedded.

The infant knows. The tight swaddling and handing off. No skin-on-skin. Wrapped and placed, not naked and held. I am efficiently changed and bathed. My new eyes search the face above me. I nuzzle against cloth, not breast. In my crib, I suck from the rubber nipple until it slips out of my searching mouth as the propped bottle slides away.

The toddler knows. I press my face into her belly and cling. An undercurrent shifts. No one sees what I sense. Outwardly motionless, her hands rest lightly on my burrowing head. My older brother hurtles into the room. I look up. The dark centres of her eyes soften.

The growing girl knows. Father does not. He sees only equality. She pours juice at eye level, ensuring identical amounts. Refrigerator art is evenly balanced: two of my brother's, two of mine. Gifts under the Christmas tree are matched to the penny in value. In photographs, she stands between my brother and me with an arm around each child. She smiles. We smile. Her hand on my upper arm bends outward from the wrist, as though holding a cigarette. Her hand on my brother's shoulder curves inward.

When the time comes, she gives me a book, *Becoming a Woman*, and a hot water bottle.

Mona Lisa
Sarah Adair

You don't touch the art.

They won't let you. Smaller than you expected, Mona Lisa sits cordoned off and behind bulletproof glass in climate-controlled conditions. She holds the Guinness World Record for the highest known insurance value in history; they're not going to let you leave your dirty fingerprints on her. Even if it *was* acceptable to fondle museum pieces.

It isn't.

You rest your palm on the rear of the cute student in front of you though, on the tight seat of her jeans. She dances away with a wide-eyed look over her shoulder. You maybe accidentally tug on the tail end of a woman's headscarf. She has no right to look at you like that; it's not like you yanked it off. You squeeze your wife's elbow and tell her to smile. After all, you came here for her.

'Honey,' you call her. 'Sweetie,' to a little girl hiding behind her mother's skirt. 'Darling,' is the security guard watching you with a frown.

More familiar than the rhythm of our own names.

You don't touch the art. The rest of us are fair game.

The Beachcomber's Daughter
Karen Jones

My eyes sift sand, shingle and silt for signs of her.

Sometimes I see her on the carousel, hair flying out behind her, a candyfloss held tightly in one hand, the reins of her horse clutched in the other, her face serious, as though she's really in control.

Or I see her paddle in the sea, dress tucked into her knickers, socks and sandals abandoned to their fate, jumping in mock surprise as cold water ripples over bare feet.

If I hold a shell to my ear I hear her skip, dance, sing a soft siren song of selling sea shells on a shore I've never seen.

I feel her tugging at my hand and my heart, begging me to build castles we both know won't stay any longer than she did.

Too early, too small, too ethereal.

I look out to sea, then back to the carousel. Will she come to me by water or revolution? Will she have seaweed between her toes or candy floss in her hair? Will she find me, or leave footprints in the sand for me to follow?

I'll wait, watch, catch, hold onto her, and this time I'll never let go.

Anna's Folly
Elaine Dillon

Emily stands at the edge of the water and watches. The four silhouettes chase each other around the folly on the cliff, their laughter bouncing off the tower and down into the bay. One of them is Anna. The others are men that Anna didn't introduce Emily to, though Anna hadn't known them when they invited her to play volleyball. Only her.

Emily didn't wear lipstick to the beach, or a halter-neck bikini with a sweetheart neckline. She didn't tip her head back and tease cherries from their stems, or sweep her toes through the hot sand like a languid cat, playfully swishing her tail. And she didn't stare at the men whose hard bodies glistened as they punched the ball backwards and forwards.

Rolling onto her tummy, Emily had wriggled to contain the flesh spilling over her waistband and pouring onto the crushed towel beneath. She read the same paragraph several times as Anna shrugged and prowled towards the beckoning men; as Anna squealed and pushed her breasts into a cleavage to spike the ball; as Anna tipped her head back when the man who retrieved the ball from the water shook droplets on her, from his shoulder-length hair.

Now Emily raises a fleshy hand in a crooked salute as the sun dips behind the ruin. The men scale the folly, each hauling themselves onto a ledge, and bending their knees before they spring into the burnt orange sky. They puncture the denim sea at an angle and surface in shards of exhilarated spray.

'Shit, it's freezing, hahaha!'

'C'mon Anna, come in!'

Emily watches Anna climb and find her balance on the crumbling edge, curling her toes into the stone.

'Do it!'

Anna reaches skyward, her ribcage rising and falling for a few beats before she moves into a crouch and stretches forward.

Emily doesn't shout stop, and she looks away before Anna's pantomime shriek becomes a deep howl on some solid place, between the air and the ocean. Gulls scream overhead, as Emily presses her tongue into a cherry and bursts the dark fruit in her mouth. Crimson stains her nails.

Breaking the Silence
Helen Matthews

A Mini Countryman pulls in. Beige-looking woman—racoon-striped hair—lowers her window. Jak ogles her as she flutters a tenner and waves away the change. We scuttle towards the car. No talking, no slacking. Mikan's last, his mangled right foot skidding on the slick, damp tarmac.

A hiss, a fizz, an explosion of spray. Four of us swarm around the Mini. Inside, the woman yawns. She's not afraid. Her car's no cage; one click of the lock and she could walk away. Not us. We're on the outside, and we're shit-scared.

If she peered behind the fly-posted car showroom, she'd see our cage: our home. Two rusting containers, a makeshift washing line strung between them, our sodden underwear dangling whenever the wind holds its breath.

Thick suds pools at our feet, seeps inside my trainers. I buff the doors, knead my cloth into a powerball and crouch beside Anja to polish the bumper. Anja's hands are pinkish-grey like uncooked tuna, and her dark hair is tangled beneath a baseball cap, but her eyes are liquid ebony.

The wind picks up. We huddle together, sheltering under the dripping, candy-striped awning. We have one yellow, waterproof safety jacket but it's Mikan's turn to wear it today. When Jak goes for a pee, Mikan pounces on a dog-end. After three puffs it singes his fingers, but he won't let go.

A black beamer roars up. The driver revs his engine and pumps the horn; his car bounces on its axle.

'Get moving,' Jak shouts at Anja, his spittle flecking her face. He grabs her shoulders, shakes her until her cap slips off and her hair floats to her shoulders like a silk shawl. 'This work too hard for you? I'll give you a new career, Princess. Not standing on your feet all day...' He swings a sodden rag towards Anja's face.

'Hey!' I snatch the cloth from him.

Jak's damp fingers prod my chest, I hear his unspoken words: *Shut your mouth, scum. You have debts to pay.*

The grit-grey sky brightens. I moisten my lips and ball my fists. Today something will break—perhaps the silence.

Bringing Home the Babies

Louise Mangos

Jude lies in the dark with her hands pressed tightly against her ears. She makes the pearly shells of cartilage creak inside her head. The ringing pressure reaches the same tinnitus pitch as the screaming downstairs. The noise echoes along the hallway and up the stairs. Jude calculates it is coming from the snug this time. Her ears begin to sweat under her hands, and instead she folds her pillow around her head. She thinks she can cancel out the sound by keeping her eyes shut, but when she squeezes them tight, stars burst behind her eyelids. Staccatos of glittering white shrieks.

Cassie has been bringing them home regularly. This is the second one this month. Jude's older sister Agnes will have awakened by now and will be on her way downstairs. Jude imagines her creeping into the snug, whispering soft words with her hypnotic voice. Agnes will spread her gentle hands, love flowing from her palms in a calming golden aura. She will gather the little thing to her chest. Silence will ensue as its racing heart slows.

And she will give it a name. She always gives them names.

She will walk serenely in her bare feet across the dewy lawn, and place it in the field for its mother to come and find it. She will wait until she sees its little white tail bobbing away in the dark.

Then she will return to the house, make sure Cassie is in her basket, and duct tape the cat flap closed until morning.

Carnations

K J Howard

I came up on the Friday. I had so much to tell him, but he told me he wasn't in the mood to talk. He was in the mood to watch TV. Two episodes and a film.

The kitchen was dirty and the cupboards bare. There were towers of plates in the sink and along the counter. Food on them stuck like moss. An abandoned city.

We ordered take-out.

*

On Saturday he wanted to watch TV again. He brought a bottle of wine and two mugs into the living room. He handed me one. It was two o'clock.

'What's this for?'

'What do you mean?'

'It's two o'clock.'

'It's a weekend.'

Silence like a knife.

'You're fucking judgemental.'

My jaw fell.

We were invited to dinner at Mickey, Sarah and John's but he said he didn't want to see people. He was lying in bed on his side watching his laptop. His bedroom wasn't dirty just strangely barren. He hadn't decorated.

When I got back, he hadn't moved.

'Are you okay?' I asked him.

'Yes.'

'I meant in general.'

'Yes.'

He pulled the duvet over his head, a slamming door.

*

On Sunday I bought him carnations. Red and yellow and orange ones. But when I got back, he wasn't in his room, and the house felt empty. I left them on his bed and went for a shower.

I dried my hair, and I dressed myself, and then I knocked on his door. He didn't answer. I pushed it open.

He had trimmed the carnations' stems and fed them into the mouths of wine bottles.

He had lined the bottles up along the ledge of his window.

Light spilt through the petals and through the glass. It looked like the sun was held inside them. It looked like I'd never seen colour before.

My jaw fell.

He was asleep on the bed. Curled like a question mark. I lay down next to him, and I wrapped my arm over him. I spooned him even though I am little and he is big.

He murmured slightly and held my hand in his.

Chimeless
Emily Devane

When, as we walk through the museum after our long-overdue coffee date, you ask me how I am, I hope you realise that my answer is not truthful. My lips form the words 'I'm fine' with barely any effort, and you comment favourably on the highlights covering my new crop of greys.

In the centre of the room is a golden clock. One of my favourite exhibits, I explain. On the hour, a cast of birds and woodland creatures spins in circles. They seem to leap and jump—quite alive—from their rising falling branches.

'I wouldn't give it houseroom,' you say, offering me a mint *for the garlic*, 'though you have to admire the craftsmanship.'

'Why not crafts*woman*ship?' You know well enough to ignore my comment, just as we ignore the awkward fact of my husband's departure. 'This was hidden away during the revolution,' I say, imagining the parts scattered, the task of putting back each tiny golden creature, each tiny leaf.

'You'd never know, would you?'

'But that's the thing,' I say. 'Though it looks the same, they were never able to make it chime. The restoration job was near impeccable, but for that.'

You cock your head to one side, and a line of comprehension crosses your face. I hope you're closer, now, to understanding that this rough approximation of a smile is little more than surface glister. Mending only goes so far, you see.

'I expect its chime was beautiful, once,' you say.

Contaminated
Elaine Dillon

The chill of the room makes him think of Miriam's skin yesterday. How he'd ran his thumb slowly along her waxy cheekbone, in a gesture that would've been mistaken for tenderness, if there had been anyone there to see. He had subtly pressed down on her jaw; an attempt to shape the smile they had given her into the thin line he was familiar with. But it was no good. Her face was as un-relenting as her mind had been.

On the drive over, he'd thought about the sitting room. The china ornaments, the taupe leather chesterfield, and the photos in their gilded frames. He'd wondered if the pictures of him would still be there. Of course they were. It would've been harder to explain their absence, and control was too important to Miri-am. Dad had said so too when he left. There was no give and take.

His room looks like it has been tipped on its side and righted again. There is one empty shelf amongst the clutter. He holds his thumb and fingers in a pinch and hops paw prints through the dust. This is where the magazines were, hidden in shoeboxes, which now sit empty on the floor.

She hadn't knocked. She'd caught sight of the man on the cover and simply removed the magazine from his hands. He'd sat on the edge of his bed and heard the bin close; the kettle boiling; a cup clinking as it was loaded in the dishwasher. Her bedroom door. He'd gone off to halls not long after.

He imagines her ransacking the room, searching for aberrant traces, her hands imbuing every object with her joylessness. Rubbing his coated fingertips together, he remembers reading somewhere that dust is 80 per cent skin. Every surface, every edge is shrouded in it. In her. Motes hang in spears of winter sun, and a singer, doubled-over and roaring into the microphone, is impaled on one. Perpetually frozen in silent rage.

Her stifling floral scent is in his nose. There's nothing to be salvaged here, but the floorboards creak with relieved tension as he takes his own weight with him.

Different Ways of Drowning
Jan Kaneen

Watching the rain dash fast against the thin window, and flashes of lightning feather the midnight sky. Trying not to think; counting to a hundred-hundred to mute the thoughts that think themselves; focussing on the rivulets that are snaking sideways on the other side of the fragile glass—so beautiful—caught by the bedside lamplight, black and silver, writhing like something alive.

*

Torrents falling harder, raging out to sea, reeling and pitching against relentless black bullets as Greg steers the hopeless lifeboat too close to the rocks. A bridge collapse at Hudson Bay, casualties to recover lost in the torrent, swept out to sea... and miles away on the other side of a window, the woman he longs for, trying to forget that he exists.

*

The downpour distorting everything as Sam Jackson fixes his eyes on the road and speeds toward the bridge. Slewing too fast around another bend, aching to get home. His heart beating the rhythm of the blades as they wash from side to side, getting faster and faster as he nears the bridge. Slow down, slow down, slow down, they seem to say, but the village-shaped lights pull him onward, twinkling like stars far into the distance through the rippling windscreen.

*

Drops of pure midnight falling slant onto neatly mown lawns. They'll be green and lush in the morning, but now they're lost lakes of black. Neatly parked cars, lit in patches by all-night porch lights, their colours leaching onto drenched angular drives, and upstairs at number twenty-four, Sonja sleeping. He told her not to wait up, said he'd be home late and not to worry, to take a tablet and go to bed, said he'd see her in the morning for eggs and coffee, and that he loved her.

*

The tumult of rain against black slate roofs, testing every crack for weakness like the dark water it is, feeling with thin fingers into darker places, into black trenches where seawater meets silt,

36

where salty pockets leave pale stains, shrouds of dirty white,
where again and again, the tide fetches up its dead.

Echo and Narcissus
Julie Evans

Afterwards, in the mirror, he tugs his penis back into flaccid symmetry. A wide stretch of broad shoulders. A roll of the neck. He goes to kiss her on the cheek and issues an unspoken command, though she is still lying in his bed, undressed. *Go now.*

Through the open bathroom door, she watches the shower jets fire at him, dissolving her scent and expunging her salt. She watches as he sloughs off, with a brush, the fine dust-veil of her skin and then, with the flat of his palm, caresses each muscle curve and dip in the undulating landscape of his body, across the catgut nerves and juts of hip.

Days go by. She waits. He fills her mind, explodes it. She texts. Texts again. *Message from Echo at 08:17. 13:31. 17:42 'Hi, just wondering...'*

At last he calls. A walk perhaps, a country pub for lunch? *Yes. Yes, please. Yes. Yes.*

The wax jacket looks good on him. The tall leather boots. Everything looks good on him.

It's late winter, and the first daffodils are blooming on the banks of the lake.

'My favourites,' he says, 'but not the yellow ones. The white ones—paper-white narcissi.' He tells her how he grows them at home in green china bowls and gives them cold vodka shots to keep them erect.

She imagines it—the shot glass, the ice-clear liquid tear-dropping on the leaves, the earth-heady perfume. Momentarily, she sees him as that flower, a floral version of a Venus trap; herself, a tiny fly teetering drunkenly on the trigger-bristle.

They stand at the water's edge. Mallards congregate hopefully then drift away leaving stillness in their wake. He drinks in the plate glass water through his eyes, transfixed.

'Come.' She tugs hard at his arm. The pub lunch beckons, a warm fire. Wine. A rustic table over which they can stare longingly. She can stare. He's un-talkative. Morose.

A fortnight passes. She dresses in silk. At the door to his apartment, she can hear him breathing beyond the spyhole's blinking eye, but he does not answer.

He does not answer, Echo.

No Smoking
Kevlin Henney

Jesus Christ, d'you see that bloke? Spliff the size of a tree, smoking like a forest fire, stoned as a mountain meadow. But running, and fast too.

No, not your Usain Bolt, but a lanky spaced-out Shaggy run, all Scooby snacks and mile-high sandwiches, bounding with parkour grace across the shopping mall, bench to bench, over grannies, under fountains, dodging buggies and bugged-out parents, a Mary Jane ballet between tempered tantrums and sulking spouses, choreographing the dance floor between Starbucks and Smiths.

Yeah, mall security huffing and puffing and crashing and stumbling, uniforms in pursuit. Sure, they look the part standing at the entrances, all badges and black shirts and don't-mess-with-us faces, but stoner boy here, grinning and toking, 'Sorry!' and ''Scuse me!', is winning gold. Never breaking a sweat, all circular breathing and aerobic chill, ash and smoke peppering and clouding his path.

Sure, your wannabe cops are jabbering into their walkie-talkies... oh, and here come their mates, Laurel and Hardy, in the opposite direction, ready to sandwich Shaggy between Miss Millies and Waterstones, but he's jumped the railing, Yo Sushi! plates flying, children cheering, parents shouting, boys in black wondering whether to make the jump... he's running the sushi track, the stolen goods under his arm.

What? No, not jeans or a camera or something from a shop, cheeky bugger's nicked the *No Smoking* signs! He's on the home straight. Now it's the obstacle course of new arrivals and revolving doors... car park... and he's won!

Foretold
Lisa Ferranti

The fortune-teller said in a past life I was a saloon dancer, a boa-clad high-stepper. She predicted I would travel by water taxi. That I'd love a man with hands hard-hewn. My mother said beware false prophets, shimmering idols, alabaster statues. I flocked to your arms of sinew and muscle, callous palms, sawdust and grit. *A carpenter?* Mother said. Like Jesus, I told her. Like your father, she said, turning a paycheck into 80-proof fast as the Son of God turned water to wine.

The angular cut of your bone, carved to fit the chink in my baby's breath armor. Mother said marry first for love, then money. We raced dusty highways, sticky grape Fanta bottles rolling at our feet. The sign said five miles to Vegas—there by dawn. Elvis said *till death do you part*, and we dodged rice rain, chased the sun.

The Lord says goodness and mercy will follow us all of our days, but at night, now, I follow you to the dingy after-hours bar on Howard Street, where I am not a dancer. I travel not by water taxi, but by rusty Taurus, exhaust sputtering in my wake. I wait in the dank alley for you to emerge, for proof. I want to lie down in green pastures. But I force my eyes wide, open the window. Hold my breath. Offer a limp dollar bill to a woman pushing a shopping cart nearby. 'Bless you,' she says.

I stroke the chained cross that loops my neck. Even before I spot you, I see the future. I start the engine, drive fast, drive east, the pink scrim of sunrise glinting off the water tower next town over, beckoning like a crystal ball.

Hair Line
Linda Grierson-Irish

Baby Blonde

'Thank you, Mr Scooter.' Mr Scooter zooms you and your best friend Pickle-pup to Plastic Spoon Planet on the other side of your neighbour's yard, where you twizzle your hair until Daddy comes home, kisses you and Mummy, and tickles Pickle-pup's tummy.

Bright Pink (should've been Sunset Orange but you left the mixture too long)

'Thank you, Mr Taylor.' You know Billy's waiting outside for you, but Mr Taylor said he'd help with your assignment. His finger-nails are so much cleaner than you remember your Dad's ever being. The next day Mr Taylor has a pink hair on his jacket for the whole class to see.

Doubtful Blonde Crop

The taxi has dropped you too far from where you need to be. At the petrol station counter, you ask directions. The male attendant is staring at the girl behind you. She has hair you could swing on. You catch two buses back home and delete your dating profile.

Unexpectedly Bald

People keep asking 'why don't you wear a wig?' You could pick any style or colour you wanted, they say. They assume you're having chemo. They assume your baldness entitles them to question your decisions. You miss your eye-brows. Your eye-brows would have told them what you think of them.

Restless Grey

Your kids' hair is thick, buoyant. Unsquashable. You conclude that your genes have done that skipping a generation thing. You tell your husband you want to move to Ireland and raise chickens. Specifically, Silver Sebrights. You love the way their feathers look like they've been outlined with marker pen.

Rebound Bald

You discover henna crowns and learn how to decorate your scalp. You draw a feather motif. It's so wonkily beautiful you try on clothes just to use the three-way mirrors in changing rooms. People ask 'why?' less often. You opt for plain or patterned, depending on how you feel.

Heritage Bald

Your grandchildren holiday with you in Ireland, where you run hair-loss awareness sessions. You weave choice into your legacy, a supplement to heredity. Together you ink an uncharted, shared universe onto your head, bordered with kisses. It lasts like a lingering embrace.

Healer
Susan Carey

Her words cast shadows. Wind chimes murmur and talismans shift in a rippling breeze. Jewel-coloured parakeets hop along perches, sensing freedom in the agitated air.

I am here because she holds my future, not my past. Her hands are covered in age spots, and crescents of garden-dirt live under her nails, but when I lie down, her touch unfurls my taut muscles and anaesthetizes ricocheting thoughts.

'Close your eyes,' she says.

Now I am dough that she may knead and roll. She will cut away fear and disease just as I gouged out potato eyes, sliced bruises off apples and scraped mould off cheese, feeding my family whose mouths were blood-rimmed caverns never reaching satiation. Abraded ropes of hunger that bound us have segued into routes taken by trains, ships and planes, leaving behind only traces of gorged fuel. Sometimes I look at the vapour trails my children leave and wonder if they are thinking of me, our thoughts crisscrossing. The ties that bind us now gossamer thin.

Her healing song is neither soothing nor pleasant but seeks an answer in the rhythmic breath of unseen mountain creatures. Benign hands follow the river of disease which has flooded me, time slinking forward; a snake shedding its skin. My eyes open and Ma Davis stands before me. I notice a grubby plaster on her finger. In the oblique afternoon light, her lucky charms are charity-shop orphans, funfair trophies gathering dust. I button my coat and pay. It wasn't magic after all, just an earthly transaction, but her blue eyes wish me well as she waves me down the mountain.

A new moon is already in the sky. I walk without limping, and the ravenous pain has gone into hiding. The healer's touch leaves a goose-pimply imprint; a crescendo of music playing on inside me. Crepuscular rays penetrate clouds above a distant range of hills and illuminate the valley below. I open my arms and whirl around, throw my face up to the sky. Joy burns me back to life. My steaming breath draws firebirds in the air, dissolving despair with the spread of their kaleidoscope wings.

Phoenicoparrus
CS Bowerman

I look down at the water frozen around my ankles and sigh. At night it gets so cold here that even the salt water in the mountain lakes freeze over. I can see my feet distorted and out of focus through the ice crystals. What temperature is this? We are trapped in the ice. Shins held tight at zero, whilst toes are un-shackled at four degrees at the lake bed. I ruffle myself above, blood circulating pink and red. A flamboyance of frothy blurs. I dreamily sniff the cold air and long for our hot mountain day to begin. Immobilised, I cannot embark on it yet, but I imagine great things, beautiful things. Eventually, the white sun drips over the peaks. The water-laughs bubble as they watch us strug-gling to escape the now porridge ice. I stretch up like I'm encour-aging a choir to rise and perform, up, up, up you go. Straw-thin legs easing out of their salty handcuffs.

Unfortunately, freedom is not elegant. I have flat feet and start an ungainly hunchbacked slithering, twiggy knees bending backwards, boater-body swaying forwards, head nodding too close to the sweating ice. But I do laugh and shriek and hold my neck high as I persevere with the battle because I know I will win. We wallow and glide, repelling the icy magnetism, grabbing our opportunity until en masse we shimmer our staccato dance across the Altiplano.

Finally, the South American sun beats down. We scorch in the flowing alkaline water, and until the night falls again, we will flirt and promenade, be magnificent and be free.

Jetsam
Sara Zkara

You wake up to find yourself the product of an overnight mutation. The thick, rough-hewn body you so devotedly donned through the sweltering summers and the endless winters is now a weightless figure that floats. Even your shoulders feel different. At this exact moment, they're just a mere set-up of bones, muscles, ligaments and tendons, and not a shelf in the lost and found where the burdens of the world are jam-packed one on top of the other, never to be reclaimed.

Not knowing how to steer this new vessel of yours, you glide from one room to the next. You crash into walls and doors. You topple a vase with a single rose. You knock over a photo of you holding a photo of you holding a photo of two talking crows.

Once in the kitchen, you shove a chopping board under your shirt. You thrust bouquets of knives down into your pants. You stack a ten-piece pan set over your head. The second your bare feet greet the glacial kitchen floor, the whole of you collapses—a heap of flesh and unused kitchenware. With fingernails dug into the gaps between the scarlet floor tiles, you close your eyes...

You dream about a soap bubble. Not a vacant flask or an empty bottle of pills, or even a drained poison vial, but a soap bubble.

'Be a soap bubble,' a voice inside your head, right then, commands.

You obey.

You drop the knives and the pans. You drop last month's bills and last year's grief.

'Keep going.'

You drop an untouched birthday cake and that time you crashed a stranger's wake.

'Marvellous!'

You drop your mother's screams and the twenty gallons of your tears.

'Gravity is only an illusion.'

You drop the days you left behind and those that still lie ahead.

'You're flying, dear.'

You drop your eyes, ears and teeth. You drop your hair, skin and bones. You drop your heart and your soul.

'Soap bubbles wouldn't know what to do with a soul anyway.'

'I am a soap bubble.'

'That's right.'

'I am the proud child of tap water and cheap dishwasher soap.'

'Yes, you are.'

Kindle
Conor Montague

'How much does that pay?'

He doesn't turn, remains stooped into the fireplace, resurrecting embers.

'Not much at first.'

Stubs of fingers coax twigs and shavings, singed sap the perfume of days together chopping. I hand him a clod of turf. He looks at it, turns it in his hand, drops it back into the basket and chooses one long and curved. It arches over the centre of the smouldering mound.

'And later?'

'Hard to know. Depends.'

He picks three short straight pieces, leans them side by side against the long curved clod, then repeats the process on the other side. Sinks onto haunches and whips off his tweed flat cap, retrieves a nipped Woodbine from behind the peak. Grabs a twig as it flares, sparks up the nipper. Acrid tobacco, sweet resin, earthy turf, scents of childhood, of manhood, of home. He exhales into the fireplace.

'That's a great word... Depends.'

Another pull. Another exhale. The fire catches, engulfing the arch. I place a couple of sods upon the flames. Bog bristles crackle. He shifts up onto the armchair, flicks ash onto the hearth before crossing his legs.

'You won't take the farm?'

'It's not what I want.'

'Good work.'

'I know.'

Two deep pulls. He flicks the butt into the fire and rises.

'You'll have a sup a tae?'

'I will.'

He plucks two mugs from the dresser, pours treacle tea, dribbles milk in that precise way of his. I add another sod as he turns.

'It's no different from working the bog, Pops.'

'How'd you make that out?'

'The digging, the spreading, the footing, the harvest.'
'Will it keep you warm?'
'Different kind of warmth.'
He passes a steaming mug.
'Will you promise me one thing?'
'I will.'
'Promise you won't turn out like that bollocks, Yeats.'

Letting Go
Lisa Mattin

I was hard and lean when we met. Fast, all muscle, no soft spots. Then we fell in love and the changes began.

I feasted constantly on your body, always starving, never sated. The salt I licked from your neck turned to sherbet in my mouth, fur encrusting the enamel-like limescale on an old kettle. I inhaled your scent, drawing it deep into my lungs until there was little room for oxygen, turning heady with its soporific effect as it stuck to the alveoli like tar. Tracing your body, constantly yearning to touch, fingerprints wore away and were lost to your skin. My lips softened and turned plump from constantly kissing but remained hungry as I devoured you, love clinging like cholesterol to the atriums and ventricles of my heart. If I could have liquidised and drunk you, I would have.

Gradually, my stomach slackened from the constant working of butterflies. I grew slow, love seeping and staining all of me. I let my muscles become flaccid so that when laying together I could mould my body to yours, my skin craving the pressure, wanting to be smothered, totally lost in you.

But love had also given me cataracts, my vision so clouded I could no longer see. The capillaries in my brain so narrowed I could no longer reason. My synapses would not work independently, they needed the electricity and chemicals than ran between us to function fully.

I was happy with the changes in me. I felt you and I were morphing into us. I was giving up one half of me so we could become whole.

I was so innocent.

At the end, when you left me and I asked why, you said, 'Because you let yourself go.'

Like an Empty Cup
Jeremy Hughes

In a corner in a café in a market town on the border, I am think-ing about the boy I loved here when I was a girl growing up be-neath the seven hills that shepherd the streets. Hills now breezed with greens which make me feel more real than I did when he took me under the ferns whose fronds roped my wrists and love gagged my mouth.

A bee as loud as a machine. The sun through a gap like a blade. The earth hurting.

In a corner in a café in a market town on the border, I wait for him. After the kiss on my cheek has evaporated like a drop of rain from a hot surface and chit-chat about what he's been doing all these years and how I haven't changed at all, there is silence between us like an empty cup I can't remember drinking before he turned up. I wait for what he'll say.

My wrists.

I bangle with each hand in turn—tight and loose, loose and tight.

The cold counter buzzes. The spotlights spear the shadow over the table. The chair is hard.

He looks down and says, *I was a boy* and *It was a long time ago*.

There are newspapers on a stand whose pages fall forward showing stories behind stories behind stories.

Flat white.

I have planted ferns in my garden and watched them turn to the sun.

Ferns unfurl their secrets, I say. Eventually.

Menace
Philip Berry

I cannot tell if the man in the empty, dusk-dulled street is walking towards me, or in the same direction. For twenty steps he occupies the hinterland of threat. Then, perceiving that he has become larger, I stiffen. The orange light thrown down by a street lamp keeps his hair aflame but his face blank. As we pass, I stop breathing. If he twitches, I will strike. I have already chosen the spot: base of the neck, front, where the air flows. He'll gag and choke. I can do it. All the energy I have is concentrated into the blade of my aligned fingers. They are sprung.

When there is space between us again, I do not relax. He may pivot, ready to slip a wire across my throat. His soft heels fade. I sneak a glimpse. He has turned a corner. He has a family, and his head is full of innocent preoccupations. I feel bad, doubting him.

Ahead, another figure. The silhouette is feminine. Her down-turned features are clear, illuminated in a bathysphere of social distraction. She lives in a world of connection, so complex, superficial. She is not aware. She cannot know if the man walking towards her is good or evil.

He is undecided.

Saturday Matinee
Margaret Meyer

Saturday matinees at the Broadway with the screen flashing white and black, a firmament of silent screen stars. Aunt Beatrice in the orchestra pit, in her element and a starring role of her own. Always wore the red crepe dress with white crocheted roses on the bodice. Liked to arrive early, smooth her music onto the stand, wave to the Projectionist. Had a habit of warming up in F Major, tutting over the piano, its top keys that stuck. Always had a box of violet creams for the Interval, she said, when she'd disappear, leaving me stalled in the stalls, all spots and bare knees, watching the watchers watch. That summer we were both overcome by Miss Gloria Swanson.

'Hark at her,' breathed Aunt Bea, 'Even when she's frumpy, she's flawless,' as we trod the path more travelled home, to Uncle Richie and his bad leg. Poor Uncle Richie. Brave Uncle Richie, who'd got a War record he'd have you know and wasn't afraid to use it. Uncle Richie had morphine and a walking stick. Aunt Bea had bruises, new ones every week.

Which she almost hid with face powder and the red crepe, before setting off for the Astoria Broadway and Saturday's matinee solace, the welcoming darkness. Until a certain autumn day and Aunt Bea, enchanting in her red and white, standing in the projector's beam, chosen by it. A hunch of mine taking shape; an inkling, arriving in a swarm of dust. Come Interval Aunt Bea exited screen left, and I did too, climbing plush red stairs with the violet creams held like a gift or a decoy all the way to the projection box. Inside, the beam cleft the dark, while Aunt Bea and the Projectionist rehearsed an unscripted close-up. Behind them, the screen said, 'Why change your wife?' The door plaque said Projectionist: F. Major.

Rita Used to Know How to Dance

Shannon Savvas

The notes are everywhere.

I am disappearing.

Squirreled amongst her sister's greying underwear.

The number of people who know I'm alive is diminishing. The number who care is even less. I include myself in the last category.

Scrunched in the pockets of pilled cardigans.

What happened to me? I serve no purpose.

Loose in the leaves of books.

When did I disappear?

In the Chinese ginger jar where Rita kept her Cadbury's Roses, *I am afraid*, encased a Peppermint Créme.

Thick with dust behind radiators.

I have no direction.

Scattered throughout the house, words, phrases, bizarre, unconnected.

Chameleon. I wear my husband like a winter coat.

Children are the camouflage he wouldn't let me have.

Nonsensical.

Rita, pita, sita, nita, dita, peeter, heater, eater, beat her,

Now watch her teeter, be neater, be sweeter.

Disjointed cries of help in pocket diaries drowned under the litter of a kitchen drawer.

I lost my voice. I lost it when I realised what I had given up. I still spoke but with nothing to say and no one to hear.

His arms and hands still excite me. When his fingers touch me, I am thrilled and pathetically grateful.

I am the ventriloquist's dummy.

I thought he was a god. I put him on a pedestal. I thought he was good. I was wrong. By the time I figured it out, breaking free was dissension, anger or bad temper. I no longer knew how to disagree.

I thought he was omnipotent.

Later he was just impotent.

How did I not know, she thinks? Her sister's voice, one she never heard. Her sister's masquerade.

Outside her brother-in-law plays with the dog.

'Get out of the garden!' The crash of his beer glass falling on the deck. 'Off the bloody roses. Rita will kill you.' A low growl. Muffled. Wet. Not the dog. It's him.

In her makeup bag, wadded to thumbnail size, its creases pink with blusher: *Now he wants to dance? After nearly thirty years of sitting.*

I no longer know how to dance.

Shift of Perspective
Nigel Tomlinson

He daydreams in the wailing van, caged between uniforms, cuffed and shackled to a hard-point. Sweat drenches him—the afterglow of pepper spray. Behind salted eyes he replays the scene and bleats his incredulity:

'She got balls, that cop. Christ. Never blinked.'

And later, as if lured by sirens, he coughs up more disbelief:

'Took the gun. Just come up and took it. Said look at her eyes. Said stick or twist, my call. Green eyes.'

She is folded against the concourse wall, shivering convulsively, though her stab vest rests against warm pipes and gold foil cloaks her shoulders. A dark stain spreads around her, and there is the smell of urine. Her shuddering sobs ricochet off every slab and beam. She is blind to the hovering faces, fails to receive their transmissions of compassion, shuns their comfort. There is no comfort.

Nearby lies the frisky French automatic, so fêted now in its frame of tape and dish of light that it mimics art. Further out on the ramp, a vague shape under plastic mimics sleep: a life now defined by a cordon of traffic cones and—a final affront—tagged 'secure'.

A hi-vis stranger crouches beside her in the wet: fifty, infinitely calm, voice like malt whiskey. He wraps a second blanket around her, draws her close and holds her tightly, sharing his warmth, absorbing the ebbing waves, breaking rules. Like her uncle Rob, twenty years before. And suddenly she is thirteen again—numbed, compliant, her green eyes unblinking and unseeing—and the spasms resume. She retches up the bad man's name.

'Don't you fret, pet, he's caught. Now, can you stand, my love? I need to get you away from here. I think your shift is over, don't you?'

Swan

Iona Winter

He kept calling me chicken-shit, forever taking liberty with his adjectives, and so my hands pushed him—hard.

Then we were devoured.

*

Mashed layers of sound filter through my ears—machines beep, and people whisper and groan. Beyond that, someone retches into a plastic container, and another rips out a fart with a bellow, 'Thank God that one's out!'

I hear my pulse deep inside me, despite an evil bastard using a pneumatic drill on a wall somewhere, and a doctor disclosing confidential details of other people, while my mind caresses the ceiling.

'The man next to you has just had a heart attack. You must be patient. We have to prioritise.'

Then I am screaming and given a shot—to shut me up like all the other women before me. What is it about my pain that they cannot stand to hear?

There is so much blood. My skin is sleek with it.

*

It must be newborns' day at the doctors' surgery, mothers and babies getting dutifully checked-up. On repeat, I am reminded of what has been taken, and of what I am not.

Some of the women look up and smile at me, but others with smoke-ringed eyes avoid my gaze, their sight cast downward to watch lines on worn out carpet squares morph in and out.

The radio announces, 'Rarotonga, seven nights, nine ninety-nine, for a limited time!'

As if any of us could manage a trip right now. How bloody cruel.

I sit at a distance—my invisible scars expertly folded away, an origami swan in an equinoctial place.

The Last Post
Letty Butler

On the day her mother died, Alice received a letter from Mr Pie informing her that she was the sole beneficiary of William Quarterstone's will. It was signed 'A. Pie' which would have made her laugh, had she not been busy vomiting on all fours.

An hour and a half later, Alice was in the attic. Two major things had happened in the last ninety minutes: she had found her mother dead in bed, the needle pushed halfway through a cross-stitch of a Labrador. She had also found the letters—forty-two years, five months and thirteen days too late. They were neatly bundled in date order, nestling in a damp corner of the leather holdall. She imagined Rosemary slicing each one open with her silver knife in a corner of the icy sitting room. It had probably been one of her many favourite clandestine pastimes, along with salting slugs and reading Struelpeter to other people's children. Each letter began 'My Darling' and ended 'WQ'. They spanned a period of twenty-three years.

When she had finished the last one, she climbed back down the ladder and went into Rosemary's bedroom. She looked into her mother's cold, grey eyes and touched her lifeless cheek—as thin as tissue. Alice pushed the needle through the Labrador's paw and pulled the thread taut. With her left index finger and thumb, she squeezed Rosemary's lips together, and with her right index finger and thumb, she sewed them shut. Eight little black loops was all it took. She left her eyes open.

Alice went downstairs and removed her clothes in the porch. She opened the front door, unchained her mud-spattered Pashley and cycled into town. At the top of Milk Hill, she dismounted. A blackbird sang as she lay down in the road.

The Line in the Sand
Tim Milner

Troy tossed a stone to Imelda; her hand grabbed it like a greedy goldfish.

Smooth, black and circular, she held it up, eclipsing the sun.

She limped down to where the sand was wet, her gait a reminder to all of the accident. Also, when she stood, you could notice that her left leg was a little shorter than the other.

Troy walked up to the line that she had drawn using the heel of her impaired limb. He stood there, his long bare toes touching the boundary that must not be crossed. She was looking out to sea, feet in the water, watching the gentle ocean as the tide drifted in. Her brown hair blew, and the waves wetted the pale skin of her calves. He wanted to hold her, to protect her.

*

The salty warmth was a long way from Chamonix and its crystalline air. Troy closed his eyes and observed the orange helicopter, lifting Imelda, cocooned in a stretcher, high into the blue alpine sky. He relived the anxious descent from the mountain, frantically phoning the hospital to be told that she had regained consciousness. Calling their mother—back in England—worried and scared.

That was the last time things were normal—even though they were not. The two of them were hurtling through the trees and then she hit one. After that, she rejected him, realized what he had led her into—risk-taking, drug abuse, liberties. He was damaged—he must reform—he knew it.

The weight of emotional pain had been diminished, even though physically she was damaged.

*

Mother called from the beach hut; it was time for lunch—potted crab, kippers, salad, home-made mayonnaise.

Imelda would sit there as part of a happy family, pretending to like him, hiding the truth.

The Reincarnations of Ellen Williams
Elena Croitoru

After Ellen's funeral, I sat at my kitchen table all day, looking out the window. Winter had stripped my apple tree of fruit and the parakeets perched on its branches had nothing to eat. Their squawks sounded like a mournful madrigal.

I waited until 1 a.m. to feed them because I didn't wish to bump into my other neighbour, Mr Cook. He couldn't stand Ellen and me. She and I used to meet for tea in my garden and read the *Private Eye* to each other. Mr Cook would glare at us, then aim his slingshot at the parakeets which pecked at the English flag he had installed next to my fence. 'Go back to where you came from,' he'd say as he looked my way. Ellen told me that, back in his youth, he used to be a member of the BNP and skinheads would get drunk in his garden.

It was now my third day of staying indoors but around noon, I heard voices coming from my garden, so I ventured out as far as the apple tree. The parakeets opened their beaks and pulled their heads back as they let out their hoarse voices. I couldn't believe it. They were speaking.

'Maria, snails are eating the palm tree,' they said. There was something familiar about that phrase. I had no idea how they acquired their speech overnight, but they reminded me of myself, back when I started learning English.

They said, 'You should get married again.' This was exactly what Ellen had told me.

Mr Cook came out into his garden but looked confused when he saw me grinning. The parakeets opened their beaks as if getting ready to speak. Their neon green feathers fluttered against a foreign, tropical breeze.

The Sideways Children

Terry Jude Miller

She takes them.

The unwanted, unborn children the town girls deem mistakes.

She places them in her eggless womb and lets them become.

The children live out there in the woods with her, in that dingy two-room cabin you can't find unless it wants you to; where the girls and boys make friends with the creatures of the forest and learn the old woman's language. They smell of burned wood and dead leaves, like their damp musk could reach right into you and pull out your heart and show it to you... show you who you really are.

They've got angelic blue eyes that cut you like a wood lathe; lay all your secrets open on the ground so people can walk by and say, 'I would have never known.'

She calls them her 'sideways children' because of how they entered the world... took a sideswipe from stupid girls with even denser boys who gave into what drives young folks mad if they don't get it. Then, when the girls are 'in trouble', the children take a detour to existence through the old woman's belly.

They grow up, you know. They become those quiet folks in the grocery store who are never impacted by the sappy music. You'll see them stare at the avocadoes trying to figure out the vegetable's angle and how they can use it to their advantage. Before you can think it, the sideways children know what you'll say; what you'll do. You want to ignore them, but it's futile; the soul's window won't let you look away. That's the fox's way of getting even; knowing why you lock your doors at night; why you leave the light on in the hall when you go to bed.

The old woman's taught them well.

The Sound of Rain on a Tin Roof
Michelle Matheson

'This tastes like cat's piss, you've never been able to make a decent cup of tea.' I nod soundlessly, not really listening.

I watch her in small glimpses. She is so much smaller. When she smiles her mouth is gummy, she isn't wearing her teeth. When I was younger, she used to take them out and chase my brothers and me around the house. We were delirious, our squeals helium balloons soaring skywards. Now, she just seems old.

My breath catches in my throat, how do I tell her? I pray to a god I no longer believe in.

'I have cancer, Mum.' Her face is an open wound. I feel my own terror rise fully formed in my throat, yet another tumour.

Then I am encased in her arms; she strokes my back as she did when I was tiny. I inhale the scent of cigarette smoke and sweet cookies. Her voice is the sound of rain on a tin roof. Each word is meaningless but together, a susurration of comfort.

'I thought you were going to tell me you were pregnant, that would have been alright.'

I can't move. She's always been opposed to pre-marital sex; she's in shock. Either that or Granny lust has her firmly in its grip.

She is the first to break, her cackle witch-like in the afternoon. I have loved her laugh all my life, and even now I can't resist its lure. We hold each other, laughing like loons, tears streaming, until we sob together on the kitchen floor.

For weeks my throat has been dusty with the need to speak. My mother passes me the cooling tea. 'Here, darling, drink your cup of cat piss, I think we need it.' She kisses my temple.

You
Alva Holland

Her mother's wedding present to us was an alabaster sculpture of a female head. It creeped me out, but I could see she had an affinity by the way she crooked her head each time she passed it.

Occupying a prime position on a shelf at the top of the stairs, it was surrounded by vivid, colourful landscape images and abstract art—vigour and enthusiasm while the head was silent, eerie and, dare I say, ghoulish.

She wore a traditional wedding dress but not in the customary colour. I ventured to ask why, to which she replied, 'I quite like ivory as a shade of the conventional, don't you?' I agreed.

Banishing all dark or coloured clothing to the back of her closet for the entire nine months she carried you, she floated through the house like a living apparition, and I got used to the monochrome. She faded into the shelf each time she passed the sculpture as if she and the female head were one.

The alabaster head began to appeal a little more.

Afterwards, she refused to wear anything except the dull blue kimono she'd retrieved from her mother's house when she was clearing out the clothes.

I didn't know what to say.

You didn't emerge all pink or any of those other bruised shades I'd heard people gleefully describe. You were the colour of the dull kimono, then ivory, bittersweet ivory. Not natural. The colour of fear, terror, grief, all the feelings.

Your box was so tiny. She didn't want anything to do with the choosing of it. I didn't know what colour to get. My mind was black, blank. Someone suggested traditional. What's traditional about this?

I chose blue, not traditional because that wasn't a thing I wanted you to become.

So many plans faded into the alabaster face. It remained impassive at the top of the stairs. I wanted to smash it to smithereens, but it was a keepsake, a memory of her mother, a person she wanted to be until she wasn't.

Spring snowdrops tease through the frozen soil where you are. New life when we were denied yours.

All the Things That (N)ever Happened to My Sister
Stephanie Hutton

I tell myself stories.

In this story, no police officers come to my door with kind faces and leaflets. They don't sit me down and say sorry as if it is their fault, not mine.

In this story, my sister's body is far, far away from the harbour waters, curled asleep. Or else, she is in the harbour but has grown a glimmering tail, then swims back up the river, laughing as she somersaults both under and over the water.

In this story, my sister Chloe is still standing on the grassy edge overlooking the water. Her left hand holds all her hurts. If I look carefully, really zoom in, I can see a miniature figure of my missing father, shaking his fist up at her. His back is covered in grey fur, his ears are pointed. Other tiny wolves encircle him and growl so gently that the sounds are lost in the breeze. They can't harm her now. Chloe closes her palm and crumbles them all beneath her fingers, then sprinkles the crumbs into the river, letting the flow carry away all her memories, so there is no need for her to jump.

In this story, I am driving up to see my sister because it doesn't matter if she is still drinking, I haven't given up on her. She knows I'm coming, so sits beside the water and doesn't take off her shoes. The only letter she writes says 'see you soon'.

In this story, my sister is safe, and I never have to miss her.

Crowbar
Lyndsay Wheble
SUMMER 2018 FIRST PLACE

Rowena had never been to the docks before. Her knuckle knocked against the shipping container—tomato red and as rusty as a bicycle—and she recoiled from the death knell that rang out. Slivers of floodlit silver sliced through the long shadows that blanketed the dockyard's secrets. She could barely see out or up. The Memorial to the Murdered Jews of Europe came to mind, which she'd visited when at a conference in Berlin. Back when climate change scientists were allowed to travel. Or work. Or think.

The dockworker spat on the ground and then crowbarred the container's doors open. He strode around inside it with his arms out like Jesus to demonstrate that it was yes, empty and yes, dry.

'So?' he demanded. She glimpsed stubble and an earring when his hooded face flashed into the light.

'Yes, fine, it's fine,' she replied, too fast. He opened the back of the van, exposing her paper darlings to the cold. Books, journals and papers stacked head-high. They had to go, Rowena thought, running her thumb down the page edges, which ruffled like anemones. No choice. Better a hopeful journey by sea than lost in a government fire.

She lifted an armful of research and placed it at the back of the container. Her ringing footsteps made her heart pound. The dockworker laughed a quiet laugh.

'Darlin',' he said, 'you know these get swung by cranes onto ships?'

'Ah,' Rowena replied, dropping her head. 'Right.'

The next stack thudded like a body to the floor. And another. And on, until the van was empty. The dockworker struck a match, and she jumped out of her skin. He turned solemn, almost tender. He offered her the cigarette.

'Some things you just don't see coming, eh?' he said, glancing up. Rowena saw him properly then: face tattoo, forties. She felt like she might cry. Her hands shook as she took a bitter drag.

'No,' she sighed. Ash flit down to the container's floor as if dirt onto a coffin. She bent down to brush it outside. 'You don't.'

Consanguinity
Fiona J Mackintosh
SUMMER 2018 SECOND PLACE

Vicodin has clenched my bowels into a fist. I grip the toilet roll holder and brace for one last burning push and, when I stand to strap on a fresh maxi-pad, a clot drops to the lino, viscous and oily. I wipe it up with a handful of toilet paper but leave the crime scene splatter on the wall for Guy to deal with later.

The rubber bedsheet is cold on my legs, but the muggy air from the window makes me sweat, so I turn the pillow over to the cool side. It smells of unwashed hair. Outside, a kid is beating on a trash can, and, every time a car goes by, the dog across the street bursts into a frenzy of barking. I slide the window shut and listen to the blood pool inside me, strident as a rusty nail, sighing in my ears, my neck, my wrists, a seashell sound, surging in the pad whenever I roll over. Three tries at IVF, then Guy was done. He said we have a good life, let's not waste it. We've walked the Great Wall, waded knee-deep in Patagonian penguins, drifted in a hot air balloon across a bleached south-western sky. In each new place, I've cupped my belly with my palms and felt it riding high, drum-tight and jumping like a cricket.

The continent inside me is bosky, uncharted. In a week they'll snip and carve and scoop, they'll split the green earth open at the source and leave a scar so raw it can be seen from space. Swaddled in a sheet, I feel the mattress dip beneath Guy's weight, the hunger in his hands, the urge to grip and pull me, fists clenched and crusty-eyed, out into the unrelenting light.

Skin

Donna L Greenwood

SUMMER 2018 THIRD PLACE

Flaps of muscle and tissue cover her face, her arms and her legs. She wishes that these epidermal remnants would disappear along with the rest of her skin. She stares with envy at the bone-bags who surround her, those for whom skin is no longer a hindrance. She admires their aesthetic. They seem lighter some-how, more efficient. They are not heavy and clad in meat as she is—they are quick and jagged as lightning. Some of them have lost their eyes. Their black-hole sockets hold an infinite wisdom that she hopes, one day, to acquire. She envies their emptiness and tries to blink out her own baby-blues.

*

At night, she picks at her skin, but the unravelling cannot be rushed. The flesh must be ready to fall; it must slide from the bone like butter from a warm knife. You cannot simply lie in bed and flay yourself.

*

It takes years of pain but eventually she is just skull and bone, as shiny and white as death. She is hard and dry, except for the nug-get of tissue binding itself inside the cavity of her womb. This too will soon be shed.

*

She is uneasy when the child raises its hand to the light, revealing an obscene redness pumping beneath the skin. She places her head to the child's chest and hears the beating of the carnal pulse. The mother weeps for she understands what pain lies ahead for her baby. Skin bruises easily; it can be burned and blown apart, twisted and torn. It can be sliced wide open and the incarnadine softness within spilled out.

Yes, she whispers, this world will be better when all skin is gone. She finds a little tag of flesh on the tip of her baby's finger and begins to pull.

Social Anxiety
Maria Alexandra

He has a unique and grounded manner of holding his coffee. In speech, doesn't stammer or think twice. I'm captivated. Bordered by the same coast from birth, he's never seen dirt tracks and rivers as silk scarves. Never breathed a prayer when cool and hot currents interlace. Never recognised that countries, like houses, have a distinct smell. Head angled with curiosity, he quizzes me about flight. What does it feel like? Do you get scared? Is it as safe as we assume?

'It's'—flat white rich on my tongue—'not what you expect. Close your eyes, and you may as well be in a car.'

I, of course, don't mention the awareness. That the earth creaks under your feet, you just don't notice until you're higher than birds. Things are closer when further apart: oceans swallowing up limestone, rain falling elsewhere, factories churning out smog. Your senses overheat from the sun, immediate and white hot with a frame of marmalade tracing the edge. Objects made of gas seem solid. And the solidarity—because truth is, we weren't given wings for a reason, but rebelled as we always do and built them ourselves. I don't mention that. No one rolls a judging eye when you turn stiff as a rock.

You can recount your life louder than ever before, no strings attached.

And because he doesn't ask about the other countries, why mention the textures of soil and people's laughs, whether thunderstorms curdle or turn to steam? Although, someone else might have.

The cafe fogs up. Outside, indistinct headlights float and elsewhere much higher, clouds part. Engines revolve, spin tirelessly, and when the landing gear descends, I remember how essential eye contact is to communication near the Earth. But he doesn't seem to be looking at me either.

'And you?' If you keep taking, they don't notice how little sense you make and the quiver of your cupid's bow. 'Are there any countries you'd like to see?'

It's our second or third date. He inhales. I've recognised by now that he likes talking about himself, which is a relief.

The Meat We Don't Eat for Love
Adam Lock

Not once in thirty-nine years.

The hamburger sits inside the opened red cardboard box, lettuce and tomato spilling out from beneath a glossy sesame-seeded bap, the edges of two meat patties sliding out of opposite sides. Not since his first date with Audrey. Mathew leans his walking stick against the plastic table, takes off his coat, and hangs it on the back of the plastic chair.

He's dreamt of hamburgers, steak in pepper sauce, pork chops, his mother's roast beef dinner with gravy, rack of ribs. He's dreamt all manner of meat carnage. But it meant so much to Audrey. Not once, in thirty-nine years, when she's asked, has he had to lie.

He picks up the hamburger with two hands, shreds of lettuce falling onto the table. He has the vague memory of his teeth dealing with meat, with the tearing and the chewing. A warm, earthy smell rises from the meat, and his jaw tightens, saliva welling beneath his tongue.

'How was book club?' he'd asked her.

She'd started to cry. 'I'm so sorry, Mathew.' She'd explained how they'd had drinks, how she and Roger found themselves alone. 'It just happened,' she'd said. 'It'll never happen again. I promise.'

Outside it's sunny. People walk past, some holding hands, others talking, laughing, but none of them takes any notice of him.

He closes his eyes, sinks his teeth into the hamburger. Not once in thirty-nine years. He chews and it's good—really good.

'Will you forgive me?' she'd asked.

He couldn't speak, only nod.

He looks up at the menu on the wall and takes a bigger bite. The animals he hasn't eaten, and the animals he will, march next to him through the restaurant, headfirst towards the bolt to be driven through the skull.

Self Portrait in June
CS Bowerman

Face with solid edges. Jaw of a flower pot. Chin starting to slacken. Hinting below. Skin is pale, shiny, the sun from the window glistening on the nose and cheek apples. Shining along lines stretching from eyes-wide to temple. Nose is straight and central. Generous but not wide. Solid. In and out. Subtle scars and freckles. Too much summer sun.

A long fringe sits like a hat close to the eyes. Dark auburn. Extending freely over the left cheek. Just tasting the ear. No jewellery. Hair nipped behind falls like bark past the shoulders. Ends stop and look back. Where did it come from? Its colour has changed.

Eyebrows frame lush, fleshy brows. Full-up and gravitationally attracted to the lids below. Spiky lashes send claws up to push them back. Resist the heavy caress! Black shadows on the lid. Then black—circles blue—circles black. Denim with gold buttons. A pinpoint target. In and out. The stare is direct.

Pass the sleepy eye baggage and sink to the mouth. Pink like a smudge. Paler above. Fuller below. The sun bright again on the lower lip. A line like a seagull crosses the path between wry turned up corners.

Which is the part that shows who I am? This is me yet already is not. Life may be flying, but here I am fixed. Here I can be who I remember me to be. Away from this portrait, I am already someone new. In and out. I blink. I turn. She has gone.

Ghosts

Lee Hamblin

He's lived in the same house for fifty-two years. Upstairs, there are two windows that catch the morning sun, and in them throughout the year hang heavy-draped curtains, drawn closed more often than open. Sometimes he peeks out to see a world opaque and cloudy, senseless with eternal unforgiving. The front door is layered thick with black paint that swells when the air is damp, and squeals like a cat-snared rat when eked open.

It can be many days without him leaving the house, and he rarely lets strangers in—only if it's someone come to read the electric meter, or to deliver his groceries. He ignores the chancers and blaggards that come knocking, watches them with tight jaw and fretless loathing until they slink away.

After fifty-two years, he knows every corner of his house, but on some nights he dreams that it has rooms he has never seen: spiralling staircases that lead to dormer-roofed attics, long, narrow corridors that end in dark, abandoned spaces, as though the house is really the size of a palace, really the home of a king. He wakes in anxious darkness, with a pounding heart, chest damp with sweat, and he questions what the dream means. The possibilities in a dream do not reveal themselves in a detuned world.

Of course, there are ghosts in this house. Many. They blow a wild and bitter chill through him whenever he has an inkling that today might be different, whenever he is told that today is the first day of the rest of his life, whenever he wakes with a lust for life. The ghosts are quick to sense his change in mood, his optimism, his slither of joy, and they rally round to crush it. The ghosts are never quiet for long, never leave him be, and he knows they never will.

Ink as Judas
Michael Salander

He won't burn his old clothes; they can go to the charity shop. As for the notebooks, he wouldn't want anyone else to see his juvenile attempts at fiction or the execrable early poetry. Back then, it was a world of pen and paper, and unless you used a typewriter, there was no other keyboard available. Now, when you look at a keyboard-created piece, it's just the words on a screen or page, but when you see a hand-written text, it reveals so much more than the words. That meandering scrawl is a betrayer, and the more illegible it is, the easier it is to read the agitated state of mind of the author. Ink as Judas. The notebooks can all go on the fire burning in the back garden. He wonders why it is that all the times he would like to remember the most seem to almost vanish as soon as he tries to focus upon them. They are disappointingly fleeting, and he can never seem to pin them down for long enough to savour them. All the experiences he wishes he could forget completely invariably outstay a welcome that they never had in the first place. When most of the detritus that represented his past has been consumed, and it's time for the years of his many diaries to go into the flames, he discovers that it's the ones with the least amount written in them that take the longest time to burn.

The Price You Pay
Gaynor Jones

You're ironing bed sheets in front of the television when he appears, all skinny jeans and bleached hair. He holds the microphone tightly, as he used to hold your hair. You had a long, dark mane which he made you tie into bunches. When the baby was born, it had a head of bushy black hair. You saw it poking out as they took it away.

And now this ridiculous bleach. You watch him flirt with the host, hold the iron away from the clothes and shoot a spray of steam at him.

You contacted his management team after a few months. They gave you a choice, more money from them or go to the papers and try your luck. But you were fifteen and already tainted by shame.

When your real child was born, the new one, your mother stood by the hospital curtain at visiting hours and clasped her hands together.

'Ah,' she said, like air released from a deflating balloon. 'Now, this is the one.'

You waved off your husband's look of confusion with a hand and an eye-roll. You tried not to remember the hospital before, where your mother towered over you with pursed lips, then blocked the doorway so you couldn't see.

He's finished talking and is getting ready to sing.

You should turn the television off, but instead you watch and press the iron down onto your thumbnail as he wails. It doesn't hurt. It's just one more scar to add to the others.

The Exchange
Elaine Dillon

Every week she tells me, you are not to look, you are not to draw attention and if I catch you looking then, so help me God, but you will feel the palm of my hand.

He's sitting down in his usual spot between the pharmacy and the Indian Palace. I think, don't look, don't look, but someone has dropped pakora sauce, and it has pooled near his feet. A polystyrene island slides along the top of the orange puddle as it creeps towards the drain.

The ridge of his spine rests against the brickwork, but there's a current that runs through his wracked body. His limbs fizzle and snap as he nods along to something uptempo inside his head, as he fixes his eyes on the face of each passer-by, follows them in a one-hundred-and-eighty-degree arc. They angle their chins at the shop windows above him.

I see him see me and he stops pulsing. Toffee stretches the teeth from my gums, and I shrivel, expecting the sting of her hand, but her head is turned towards the road. His face is all ripples and twitches. He rocks his heels forwards, flattening his burst trainers against the ground. The tang of pakora sauce and bitter-hop sweat is in my nose.

I think, stay still, please stay still and quiet. If he moves, she'll know I looked. I meet his eyes, stare straight into them with my silent plea. He could choose to betray me at any moment; he could pitch himself forwards and lunge at me, take me hostage in a bony cage of limbs. I try not to blink.

When I'm right beside him, his bristly jowls sag, and he brings his palms together into a slack bowl. I keep walking, but when I'm far enough beyond him and suspicion, I take a toffee from my pocket and drop it with a backswing of my arm. The wind scuttles it along the pavement behind me.

I wait ten seconds before I dare to look back. He's wearing that big wicked grin again as he slips the toffee into his pocket.

The Artist's Model
Susan Carol

Emilie fine-tunes his pulse with every brush stroke. His figure on the chaise longue, mere game plan.

Mid-afternoon, early spring. Sunbeams insinuate dusty nooks despite the well-swept wooden floor. Tins of brushes rattle slightly, victims to a sturdy breeze from the skylight. The wide sash windows facing west remain calmly open. The walls, camouflaged by sprawling canvases, some hung some stacked, a tall mirror, an antique wardrobe stashed with throws, cushions, drapes. But our eyes are ever drawn to the centrepiece.

Emilie carefully fleshes skin onto his cheeks, layers background shadows, dancing shafts of light, delineates the provenance of each hair follicle on his loins. Rising from the once blank canvas, a superb being comes to life.

For Emilie, it is like falling in love. Discovering contours, rhythms, nuances, in an unfolding of self-expression. Emilie does not believe in love at first sight.

She favours the earthiness of oils, their calibrated flow, their stickiness potential, their textural capacity. Their grainy smell and the sharp turpentine stench of day's work done.

When the model moves, he does not change. This proves to Emilie that her developing creation is the real thing, its model a mere shadow.

I only come into the light when I paint, thinks Emilie.

It's getting dark, and Emilie hates painting without natural light. It skews her palette, brazens hushed tones so that the next day they are not in harmony. That's the way to create monsters, chimeras neither of day nor night.

Dusk falls and the young man rises at her command. She doesn't know his name, or maybe she's simply forgotten. It's immaterial. He's a good model. Gustav recommended him, and Gustav knows what she requires.

She closes the windows against the chill night air but opens a fanlight. Washes the brushes, cleans the palette. Hangs her apron, unties her hair. Grabs a shawl and leaves for Gustav's.

Gustav favours artificial light and, also unlike Emilie, has one single muse. He pays handsomely. Night work suits her, and she tolerates his attachment.

One day, he often jests, I will sit for you. Emilie smiles as if humouring a small child.

Collapsing Isosceles
Lucy Goldring

'Oh yer—it's *totally* uneven! Look at her right eyelid, there's a weird extra fold.'

Real beauties, these best friends of mine—the female one, and the male one that I love. She's all caramel locks and Julia Roberts smiles. He's tall, tanned and spaniel-eyed.

Aged twelve, we had formed the perfect isosceles. I held it together at the bottom: solid and strong. They flirted at the apex; slanting out like a well-made tipi.

But at fifteen, my asymmetry surfaces—and delights. Scrutiny nutrifies their beauty-bond. They're standing hip-to-hip at the top of the kitchen, perfect cheeks propped against the pine effect worktop. I give it the am-I-bothereds from the knee-high pew below.

Our configuration is at breaking point. I know they want to parallelise... get horizontal.

So they do. Twice. But the earth doesn't move, if she's honest: too 'fumbly' during; too needy after. She calls it off, casual as that.

Three heartbreaks later, he chooses me—it's like coming home, he says—and for six years he settles.

Now she's back. Humbled by heartbreaks of her own. Kept us on the radar—easy nowadays. Couldn't *believe* her two school besties had got together. He's different, isn't he? So *confident*.

They're aligning their elbows on my dead uncle's table. Watching them talk is exhausting: an echo chamber of conceit. I'm reflected a thousand different ways, not one of them flattering.

Something shatters out of earshot. Maybe my heart or maybe just our mirrored bedroom wardrobe (he knows his best angles).

Who am I to come between them? Let them snap into one perfect line. I'm already spinning off, a twirling baton blurred against the blue—

He's exquisite, my new beau; a real gargoyle. For months we've swapped wonky grins on the 8.03. I can't wait to embrace my ugly side.

The Bell Witch
Courtney Harler

The empty sugar bowl. The cracked milk pitcher. The sticky mess of sweet. The pudding, the offering, no one can eat.

Because the witch, she concocts it. She steals it from the cane, the cow.

She bites my neck until I taste blood, running and pooling in my belly like cider.

I'm made drunk with fear.

She cackles with the crows in the sky, swirling.

She wrenches my burning ears until they pop off.

Mama! I squeal.

You naughty! Ring that bell again and just watch—I'll let her get you.

*

I drape the mirror with a quilt before sleep. I'm cold in the attic, even with the warm chimney bricks. The pale wallpaper is peeled back in jagged triangles, like missing eye teeth.

I doze and a weight gathers against me. I open my eyes to see a black cat on my chest. She exhales, I inhale. Her breath is rank, rotten mice caught in a snap in the walls of the attic. She says, My sweet, and her voice sours into a crow's—mocking, biting, bitching, bleeding.

Mama, I whisper.

Mama...

*

I am dead and Mama weeps.

But I see her, the witch.

She transforms me.

I am feline. Avian.

I peck at Mama's crying eyes.

And then I sleep.

When I wake, Mama's here.

She says, You naughty. I told you, you naughty.

What else could I be?

Be a girl. Be alive.

But I rang the bell.

I know. You naughty.

Roadkill

Rupert Dastur

Toby picks up the squirrel by its bushy tail.

'Daddy,' he says. 'Look!'

The squirrel has been flattened by a vehicle, its body papyrus thin, mummified with mud and muck, dried gore smearing its grey fur. Death's bloody signature. Its eyes are crow-plucked, and long teeth show in a macabre smile.

My son dangles the dead animal from his delicate fingers, appalled by his find.

'Should we bury it?' he asks, as if something of the squirrel has passed to him, some sequestering, survival instinct. The hiding of things underground.

'Put it down,' I say.

He lays it on the floor, reverently. I walk over, pull out a small bottle of sanitising gel and wash his hands. I scrub and scrub and scrub.

'Daddy,' he says, 'you're hurting me.'

I stop.

Birds shrill in the leafless trees.

'Let's go home,' I say.

He jumps in frozen puddles, kicks stones, searches for sticks which turn into knightly swords. We battle demons.

I teach him that the sun rises in the east and sets in the west. I point to the last of the day's lengthening light cresting the church. I tell Toby that his name means *God is good*.

At home, we slip out of autumnal clothing and into pyjamas, dressing gowns, and slippers. I make Toby a hot chocolate which he fills with marshmallows.

Later, I tuck him up into bed and kiss him goodnight.

'School tomorrow,' I say.

My son exhales, a grown-up exhaustion.

Downstairs I wash the mugs, wipe down the table, sort the dirty clothes into light and dark, write a Monday to-do list, and then collapse in front of the TV, letting the bright, squawking images silence my thoughts.

It is late when at last I climb the stairs. As I reach the landing,

Toby opens the door of his bedroom and stares at me sleepily, his eyes like half-moons.

'Did Mummy look like that?' he asks.

He yawns in response to my unprepared pause.

'We should have buried it,' he says.

He shuts the door, disappearing from view, leaving me alone with his verdict and the softening sound of his footsteps.

Some Other Place
Jupiter Jones

Alibi; from the Latin meaning elsewhere. That's exactly what I need now; to have been elsewhere, some other place.

Where I shouldn't have been was Seabank Road, where he lives, lived, used to live. Not there. Absolutely not there, or anywhere between there and the coast road heading south through the sand dunes. Those unmapped marginal spaces, soft, unstable, shifting, shiftless, dry as bones. Not quite land, not yet, just a bit of the sea that the tide doesn't reach anymore. The sand comes pouring over the top of your shoes, into your mouth, your ears, your nose; you could drown in it. I know that now. Somewhere out there is where I was conceived, in some dip, my feckless dam with her knickers off, amongst tufts of marram, tough as hawsers, sharp as stilettos.

A local boy you might say.

Further inland the sand gives way to marshland, sour and flat, and after that, the county properly begins with honest-to-goodness black earth that you can put a spade in. There, you could dig a grave, deep and plumb. But not in the dunes. Even with a spade, I couldn't have made a good fist of it. It's all dry as bones.

So I scooped out a bit of a hollow and rolled him in. Then I scooped the dry, dry sea over him, scooping and shovelling with my arms and my cupped hands and scuffing with the sides of my feet. And I wept like a squonk, yet my tears didn't wet the sand or trickle into my mouth but dried instantly on my hot skin. I hated leaving him there, but what else could I do? We had gone on my push-bike, me standing up on the pedals and panting. Him behind on the seat with nowhere to put his feet, just sticking them out either side, and the hem of his dress flapping, and his arms tight around my waist, and both laughing, laughing with a pocketful of lust and an onshore breeze in our faces.

But sand shifts. Sands shift. Now it's just a matter of time.

Da Vinci Would Be Chuffed
Judith Wilson

My hero product is continental.

Butter, that is. Until the advent of my tiny masterpieces, chiselled minutely onto each pliable block, I'd always pick the supermarket bargain. Now I'm a connoisseur. Everything counts: colour, density and texture.

I've experimented widely. Salted versus unsalted, organic and even goat. But the best is European, its raw, unpasteurized cream delivering the palest hue.

It's the perfect ivory canvas.

My knife dives in, sharp-tipped.

We all have hobbies, right?

Mine began with a few scratches whilst I was bored at breakfast (the kids were staying over at their mum's). I doodled with a toothpick on butter, instead of paper and a pen.

(I'm a graphic designer. Got an A* Art 'A' level. I can sketch a bit.)

First time, a stick man, morphed into a witty self-portrait.

Second time, a cartoon dog for Joe, capturing its canine swish.

Third time, a copy of Tilly's doll, including her cute dress.

Then—what can I say? Obsession set in. Sounds daft, but I copied a Warhol. The Marilyn Monroe one, with her strong lips and wavy hair.

The slick silhouette on dairy worked a treat.

Then it was a short hop to the classics, down the centuries. I started with twentieth-century abstracts, Picasso and Mondrian, finished with seventeenth-century Vermeer. (*Girl with a Pearl Earring* was a particular success.) Now it's sizzling June. I have to stand with arms outstretched into the fridge, to stop my canvas melting.

With Mona Lisa, I've reached a pinnacle. Da Vinci would be chuffed. Like all artists, I tinker to finesse it, unsure whether I'll ever be done.

Sunday night I order a takeaway—I'm too busy crafting to shop.

I get food poisoning.

(The kids are in Greece holidaying with their mum.)

I've been two days in bed, sick as a parrot. Mrs P from next door lets herself in. Stands in my bedroom, hands on hips, all concerned.

'Cuppa?' she asks.

Mrs P returns triumphant, announces: 'Tea and toast!'

I gaze aghast at the creamy globules spread with love.

Watch helpless as one-eighth of Mona's face dissolves.

She's smiling though.

Three Down

Charlotte Newman

Three sisters lived in Seven Sisters.

Three down, four to go!

That's what Father said.

They grew up in a flower shop. Mother never cut their hair, though she'd always scissors to hand.

Snip, snip! Weeds out, moon's out! Plants fed and in their beds! Now, a big juicy blossom for my little blossoms!

And she gave them each a flower: a lily, a rose, a poppy.

Fat-blossomed girls, you make the rockin' world...

Father liked to sing.

Mother worked hard, was swiftly sick, and died on the birthday they shared.

Four weeks passed. Lily travelled, Rose studied, Father went away with water in his eyes—but Poppy stayed home.

Poppy, the baby blossom.

Her face when they all returned! Joy like a sweet cherry moon! She could have danced and did a bit, right there in the shop; the agapanthus trembled in time. Lily laughed and Rose smiled, something Rose did often. And Father was home, spritz-fresh, teeth white as daisies! They were relieved to see that smile.

Well, well! Three down...!

Four to go!

The response was their duty, they knew.

Lily said no one in the big round world had heard of Seven Sisters, which made the joke harder to carry.

But Father wasn't listening.

Girls, I've some news.

There was a woman outside the shop; it was Mary, who gave them manure. Manure Mary. She waggled her fingers, and the sisters waggled back, tentative, swaying ferns.

Mary!

In the doorway, she lingered like she feared bad spells.

Come in, Mary!

Father insisted.

Mary patted her lavender curls, sniffed and obeyed.

There's room for four in our garden.

Eyes on the suitcase she clutched in her hand, a suitcase patterned with flowers.

Father beamed.

Mary's going to move in. For a while.

Lily said nothing. Rose's smile slipped. Mary cleared her throat, and that was her first mistake, Poppy would later think, the wet squelch of her gullet.

I hope you'll think of me as a sister.

That idiocy was her second.

But the smile that followed, the oily smile. That was the third and the worst.

Poppy reached for Mother's scissors, so good for getting weeds.

Caught in Time
Brindley Hallam Dennis

Two rusting tractors on a fellside above a lake, one perhaps pre-war, the other thirty years younger. Side by side, but not facing quite the same way, somebody must have driven them, or maybe towed that second one, on their last journeys to this resting place of sorts.

And the village walking group pauses, to take in the view. Some of the men clamber over the old machines, joke about having them running in an hour or two, something the farmer couldn't afford, or wouldn't care enough to do. Massey Fergusson, someone says. Fordson, another observes. It's important to show they know what these things are, that they still care, still feel the power implied.

Then, across rough pasture to the wall where an awkward stile slips the path over and down greasy stone steps, where he stops and stands, holding out a hand to help the others over one by one. And she, coming last of all, takes his hand but still manages to slip. They make a tango couple's move, she almost on her back, he bent forward with her in his arms, and he stares down into eyes that usually freeze him out. She's not his wife. But this time for a moment, seconds long, she lets him in. There beyond reflected blue and white-puff clouds shine stars, nebulae. He feels the pull of the earth's swirl, heartache, and not the coronary type.

Not his heart though. He has made his play long before and been rejected. Today, he would have caught anyone, even her husband, that way at the slippery step. Everyone has stopped to look. His eyes reflect like glass. She sees her own softened look turned back, struggles to her feet.

Thank you, she says.

You're welcome, he replies.

They all walk on, down the narrowing path.

A Ghost Story
Laure Van Rensburg

I became a ghost around the same time people became shoes. I sit on the ground curved spine, eyes riveted to the sidewalk. They walk past, trendy trainers, high-heels, black brogues, old and new, all sizes. They never slow down as they pass.

I used to be a person, I had a job, a flat, I stood straight. Then I lost one, and it wasn't long before I lost the rest, myself included. The streets took the little colours left in me, and I melted into their background.

Today, I'm haunting a corner of Charing Cross Road, invisible amid a crowd, on my square of bin liner, the only protection between me and the biting cold of the pavement. A group of sandals saunters past, glittery nails on display, followed by a hurried pair of dress shoes, all intent and confident steps.

I'm blowing on fingers as numb as the rest of me when a pair of little red patterned Mary Janes stops in front of me. Their shiny tips face my direction, two little arrows pointing at me. I lift my head away from the constellation of chewing gum stuck on the pavement to discover a little girl, looking right at me. I see myself in her big blue eyes, I still exist. She holds out her fist with a solemn look, unwavering until I open my hand. She leaves something in it. She smiles at me, and the tears well up in my eyes.

'Thank you.' The words croak under the rust of my unused voice.

She runs off to join her mother, leaving me with a goodbye giggle that lingers long after she's gone. In the centre of my blackened palm stands a heart-shaped sweet—red translucent glucose on a fluffy white base.

Freefalling

Dettra Rose

In the circus of my mind, I'm backflipping in tight imperfect circles. Tumbling. My spine a perfect arch. The world turns in giddy hoops, and the audience applauds. In the circus of my mind, I'm juggling clubs—three, six, then nine. Quick time, my clubs become sharp knives. The crowd says, 'Whoa!' I bow, then climb the trapeze. My apprentice hands me the swing. I freefall. Flying with no harness in the peaks of the marquee where God lives.

In the circus of my mind, big cats, elephants and proud horses are always uncaged, always unharmed. They visit the marquee, but nobody holds their reins. I ask them if I can ride bareback, no harness. Out of the canvas, into fields with no tracks or paths, we disappear.

There is a tear. There is a soft shudder in my ribs. There is a metal taste in my mouth. There is a harness pushing me together. I'm all buckles and belts. There is a view of white above me. I've seen nothing but white for weeks. Like I'm in a snow shaker.

Because when your mind's a circus, backflipping, juggling clubs and knives. When tightness squeezes out your breath. When your heart is busy numbing out what you feel, and your mind's tumbling. When you look ahead but can't see the road or hear the turning wheels.

It's easy to backflip. To turn in giddy hoops. To fly with no harness—freefall. To lie in the gutter and look in the elegant eyes of a stranger. Perfect. Bronze. Almond eyes. It's easy to like his questions and gentle care. To feel the hand on yours is warm. To hear a hi-lo siren and know it's here for you. To look up at a ruby grapefruit moon and wonder if it's the last thing you'll see then perhaps it's here for you, too.

And there are faces in your mind. And all the ribbons that cut you start to fray. And you wish you'd said what you really meant to when you could.

This is Why We Didn't Have Sex Last Night
Rupert Dastur

Last night I was in bed with my boyfriend, and because it was warm and we were feeling frisky, we were naked and wrapped in each other's arms, enjoying the solidity, the weight and the closeness of one another. My hands ran across his body, fingers firm against his skin as if I could bury myself into him.

And then I felt something small and circular among the hairs of his chest, like a spot or a mole and so I peered close, my chin resting by his left nipple, trying to ignore the hardness of him as I carried out my examination.

You should get that checked out, I told him.

Perturbed by the uncertainty in my voice, he sat up, switched on the bedside lamp, and began his own skin scan.

I've not noticed that before, he said.

I slid from the covers and went to the toilet, and when I came back, he was standing close to the light. His cock had become flaccid, and he'd put his glasses on.

It's moving, he said.

I came close, my hand on his shoulder. I squeezed a little, to let him know I was still in the mood.

No, it's not, I said.

Look properly, he said.

So I looked. It had six legs that wriggled.

What the fuck? I said.

It's a tick, he said. He took a photo of it on his mobile before squashing it between forefinger and thumb. Back in bed, we scrolled through Google.

You could get Lyme disease, I said.

Unlikely, he said.

He put his phone away, and I closed my laptop, and then we snuggled, although our earlier energy had dissipated.

I wonder how you picked it up, I said.

He yawned. Probably Richmond Park, he said.

He held me tight, and I felt his warm breath against my ear. I pictured the tick, the way its jaws clung to him, secreting toxins that would cement it in place until it was gorged.

My love, I said, when were you in Richmond? He didn't answer, and so I lay there hoping, desperately hoping, that sleep was the cause of his silence.

The Book Girl
Ian McGlashan

He first saw her sitting on a station platform. Not on a metal bench with grey paint peeling to reveal the old red beneath, but cross-legged on the concrete. She was reading a Discworld paperback. His mates approached her; he hung back, feeling shy. They were heading to a bar in town, pressing her to come with the promise of free drinks. She resisted, but he could see she was tempted. She wore a white vest-top and grey combats, with Converse boots which had seen better days. Her bobbed hair gave her a boyish look, and her face was... not pretty exactly... cheeky.

She went with them. Drinks were bought and passes made, but she wasn't for sale. His mates gave up, moved on. He stayed, awkward but hopeful. She took his hand. They left the bar.

The bedroom in her flat was too stacked with books to sleep in. A single mattress lay along one wall of the kitchenette, raised to knee-height on more books. There was no other furniture, only a wicker laundry basket containing underwear and a green inflatable dragon. She gave him Bailey's in a pint glass; he sat on the mattress expectant, nervous. She said, 'Let's go to the park.' Disappointment mixed with relief: 'Okay.'

The park was a silvery cliché in the moonlight. She said she came here at night when she couldn't sleep; he said it was unsafe alone in the dark. She shrugged: 'Doesn't matter—I can't be hurt, I'm already broken.' He held her gaze: 'I can help mend you.' She looked up at the moon, smiling, eyes glistening: 'No one can do that.' He said nothing, just squeezed her hand, resolved to try.

Back in the flat, she stripped to her knickers, asking him to lie on the wall side of the mattress: 'I don't like to feel trapped.' She slept. He lay cramped and still, not wanting to wake her, savouring the moment despite his discomfort.

Later she woke and cooked breakfast, which they ate under the duvet. Toad-in-the-hole. She couldn't find any gravy.

A Natural Conclusion
Hannah Clark

It does not take long for the plants to take over. First it is the weeds, charging into the cracks between brick and mortar without hesitation. They curve into the scattered sunlight beside you and warm their necks against your skin. Then come the creepers, tendrils reaching upwards to embrace dusty banisters and grip cupboard handles with an authority no one could have predicted. They caress your ankles and squeeze your knees, holding you tighter as you shrink.

Time slicks past you without disturbing what is left. Finally, the thistles arrive and edge up through the flooring, their roots are deep but so are yours. You do not move for them, and so eventually they move through you.

At the end of summer, when the season is ending and days are shorter, the cabins are emptying up and down the mountainside; finally, inevitably, a person comes. They are horrified by your strange new beauty. They place a panicked phone call, and flashing lights attached to racing vehicles bring more astonished onlookers. You are resplendent, and your slender novel nestled in the printer tray tells your story with an eerie precision. Right down to the thistles.

You filled the space between your cabin and the earth with soil and seeds. To the sound of pages printing, whispering and fresh with new ink, you welcomed the bees who you had spent so long befriending, and in turn they brought you variety on golden coated legs. You drank the medicated wine carried all the way from your cellar at home and combed your fingers through the grey lengths of your hair as your eyelids grew heavy. Then you laid your body on a bed of compost and let flora claim you and with you, the sickness that had stolen both breasts and your left eye. You had always loved the earth, and if you were to return to it early, you would do so in your own way.

'Suicide,' say the papers.

'A natural conclusion,' counters your novel.

Force, Mass, Freedom
Stephanie Hutton

The bathroom scales clunk their judgement as I step on naked, swaying on tiptoe for no sensible reason. The man at the coffee shop with a whipped-cream voice told me *weight is a force*. I wrote that phrase on the front of a notebook and felt the heavy truth of it in my hand.

Despite all my efforts, the red needle points to the same number as ever. It doesn't add up. Those calories I burn each night, shaking in half-sleep from memories that turn to sweat on my skin before I can grasp them. I ache with the effort of heaving, cleaning, not crying for the old people in the care home six days a week. When my mother calls, I pace the bedroom and scrunch paper into balls as she lectures. I scrub the kitchenette and bathroom until the early hours, avoiding my bed and thoughts. This amount of effort needs energy, needs food. It should balance out.

Mass is how much stuff is in an object. I googled it. No aunt asks me what my *mass* is, reaching over to pinch my flesh and inquire if I have a boyfriend yet. What's crammed inside me? Sticks and stones. Guts bursting with rejection. A heart heavy with the sighs of my mother. Every sharp-edged consonant and pitying vowel I collected over twenty-three years of survival.

I layer my clothes back on and lean against the porcelain basin, panting. Dizziness from leaping up causes a strange sensation. I'm already lighter. I drift to the bedroom and open the window, clinging to its frame to stop my body floating right through.

A long, vibrating note pours out from the back of my throat. An opera of oppression. Crotchets, quavers and minims glide upwards. Dangling from each note: a stick; a stone; a bead of rejection; a droplet of my mother's breath; every letter of every word spoken in jest or attack or sympathy.

A new force tingles through every molecule that matters. I wrap my arms around myself to embrace my freedom.

I Left the Train
Gordon Simms

I left the train, after an eight-hour journey, at 2.00 a.m., with no choice but to walk the nine miles home. I'd often done it when at school, but not with a full rucksack and waterlogged boots from scrambling all day on the slopes. Not being a climber, I was directed to plough through one snow-filled gully after another. The girl had been found at dusk, having fallen four hundred feet into a crevasse. Two nights previously, back at the climbing club's hut, she'd won a raffle. The bottle of champagne stood untouched in the cupboard.

In those days it was rare to appear on television, but I turned away from the camera as it pointed toward the stretcher and the mountain rescue team's bright yellow land rover.

My spirits lifted when a patrol car pulled up alongside; a few miles in the warm before being dropped at my door would be some small compensation. Then I recognised the driver. Now a sergeant, he'd been the school bully. He didn't readily accept the explanation of my tramp-like presence in the small hours. When I told him he would be able to read the story in the bloody Daily Mail, he closed the window and accelerated away, the rear lights dwindling to nothing in the pre-dawn blackness.

Gone

Elaine Dillon

I haven't started the search for you today, but I find you on Google Maps. Virtual me stands looking at virtual you as you peg an army of shirts to the line, white snapping against blue. A good drying wind, you'd say.

When I zoom, you melt into a creamy streak. There's a vanilla cable-knit in your wardrobe, and I press my face into the wool. It smells of your body lotion. Oatmeal and shea butter. There's an ivory bathrobe too, but that's not what you're wearing in the picture, because only slovenly women go outside in their nightwear.

Until two months ago. Your face was shadows and uncertainty beneath the streetlight, as I slipped my arm under yours. You hadn't worn your slippers, so you sat on the edge of the bath with the water around your ankles, smiling and stroking my hair, as I scrubbed your blue feet pink. I smiled back, relieved you'd forgotten that this was your vision of shame.

The policeman, the one who showed me the security footage of you leaving the bank only minutes after me, says it's unlikely you're still alive. He sits with his knees apart, feeding the peak of his cap through his fingertips. I tell him again that I was tired. He says he knows. He's sorry, and I know he's thinking about the day you disappeared when he chuckled and told me that new mothers forget their children all the time. I'd asked him if he knew whether children forgot their old mothers too. He'd looked wounded, as he does now, when I straighten and remind him that they haven't found your body.

I wish I'd thought to ask you where you were going, those nights you left the house. Those nights when you forgot about me too.

I crawl my daily spiral outwards from the town centre until I find myself back at the last place you might remember as home. Against the greying sky a nightdress billows and a sleeve rises, pauses, in a wave. If I squint, the woman taking in the washing looks a bit like you.

98

Breathe
David Rhymes

Face down in the pool, you watch the light stir on the tiles, re-membering a dark night when it snowed, around the back of old Saint Xavier's church, a boy whose neck was warm, whose hands were cold, who pressed in close and joked—the ghost of Mary Howlett, much-loved wife of George, come back to life and skit-tering between the stones—and you two kissing in the dark, fol-ded into one another then, some twenty years before, forgotten until yesterday, when wheeling out the lunch cart, down the aisle en route to Abu Dhabi, a passenger reminded you of the sweet way he cupped your chin in his two hands, one snowy night when your eyes snagged, and all the memory rushed through you then, so now when you are floating face down in the pool at the Rashid Hotel, doing an overnighter, drifting with those other strangers and their children diving in like seabirds chasing coloured rings, and you there with your face washed wet with tears, remember-ing the night your heart was gifted in the snow, a smile that shook the ghost of Mary Howlett from her grave and got her on her feet and dancing.

Please, he said, just meet me once. Once. One drink.

You wanted so much to say yes. But James, you said, you know what this might mean. I love my sister much too much. I won't. I can't.

How can you stand there and say that? he said, I just don't un-derstand. And, Please, he said.

I can't. I won't.

But how long now before you have to lift your head and breathe? You with your husband back in London and your sister's husband on your mind? How long before you have to breathe?

The Appointment
Emma Neale

In the hospital's eye department, there are two identical artworks framed on the wall. 'Why?' asks my seven-year-old.

'Perhaps it's like a game of spot the difference,' I answer. 'Or an eye department joke about double vision?'

'A super-bad one,' he says, giving me The Look.

We wait ages. Our books get tiring, so we start a game of hangman.

On the third round, my son finishes the gallows just as a young, handcuffed detainee is ushered in by two cops. My son's hand freezes over the paper as the trio disappears behind a partition.

'J?' I guess, pretending all is normal, so my son won't be afraid. He draws a blank head.

The men reappear. 'FUCK that,' says the jailbird.

'Language,' warns the short cop, as they escort the prisoner to the men's, where they have to wait in line.

'Ps and Qs,' I whisper. 'Mind your Ps and Qs.' My son looks puzzled.

'I?' is my next guess.

He pencils in another small circle.

'An eye for an I?' I ask. He throws The Look again. Then, in his clear, piping, piercing way, he asks, 'Are the police here 'cause justice is blind?'

I glance at the tattoos that flick like blue blades up the pale skinhead prisoner's neck.

The room plays deaf.

My son's name is called like a lifted sentence.

Hands-On
Adam Lock

In spring, I climb trees.

My hand is small in Dad's ginormous hands. I don't speak because I'll cry. Dad lifts my hand to his mouth. The bristles of his beard are rough. His teeth nibble. A sharp sting and I pull my hand away, hold it to my chest. Dad grins like a chimp. Between his front teeth is the splinter. He takes it from his teeth and shows me in the palm of his hand. He asks for my hand. I show him, and he kisses it.

In summer, Dad helps me build a new bedroom.

I prepare the mortar in the mixer, shovel it into a bucket, climb the ladder, and empty it onto the spot. With his trowel, he slices it, scoops it, and flicks it.

'Perfect,' he says.

Gail, pregnant, shouts from the bottom of the ladder that dinner is ready.

We sit on the scaffolding, looking out across the estate. Dad uses the end of his trowel to spell out the date in the mortar that will be hidden beneath roof tiles. He hands me his trowel, and I add our surname: Fellows.

In Autumn, I watch Dad fastening Ewan's coat, trying to push the large wooden toggles through each buttonhole. Ewan, his chin on his chest, watches his grandad's fingers.

'There. Off you go.' He pats Ewan on the shoulder, only half his buttons fastened.

Ewan kisses his Grandad and runs through the school gates.

In winter, hospitals are bright places.

'Take it out, Michael,' Dad says, his hand shaking, showing me the needle.

'Can't Dad. You need it.'

'It hurts. Take it out, Michael.'

The needle is crooked, hardly in his flesh at all, white tape flapping loose.

'I'll get a nurse.'

'No,' he says. 'You do it. Hurts, Michael. I'm tired.'

I look around for a nurse, but there isn't one. I hold Dad's hand, and his fingers curl around mine. With my other hand, I pull the needle out from between his silver-skinned knuckles.

His shoulders fall, his breathing slows, and he's asleep.

I kiss the back of his hand and place it on the bed.

A Life
Paul Negri

...fast flowing, dragged by the hair, filled with fear and wonder, beyond the point, cry from a dry throat, salt sun burning and black beneath so cold, shivering and Mommy and the towel with starfish, wrapped up like a papoose, Aunt Caroline laugh laugh laughing, a hard breathing, so tired, second-floor walkup, bread and butter, Joey crying, move the arms and kick, come on, head under and gulp gulping ocean

soccer, bad skin and Mr Peachionni hit by the car, grief counselors, Joey joking, laughing, oh God, and bleeding the first time, burning, so scared, razors in the lungs, sink sinking like a stone

Dad gone and Mom in Ithaca crying in the dorm, Richie with black hair and the war, body count on TV, wetting the wetsuit, oh not now, come on, not this, the twins in the twilight sleep, no pain, no gain, not sorry, not now, down but not out

flap arms, scare sharks, think you're a fish, a mouthful of water, sea urine, fish fuck in it Richie said, W. C. Fields Richie said, sick from chemo his hair gone, oh Richie, the twins double wedding, so beautiful, looking down from heaven, like hell, oh God, float, no stroke, come on, lazy Aunt Caroline said, no, just tired, go to hell, leave me alone, don't leave, Richie

Ashley, my first, gone just like that, like an angel from God, Ashley to ashes, Botox, stupid old woman, what a waste, swim alone at dawn, you never listen, it's okay, so sorry girls, don't cry for me Argentina, so cold, brain freeze, okay, let go let go let go, so dark and deep, wrapped tight, her face, Mommy and the towel with starfish...

Give & Take
Dan Tremaglio

Tell me your name is always how it starts. Hours later it ends in the barracks on a couch in the dark. The one who asks is the one in power. They are not even half naked. They met in the officers' lounge and decided and wasted no time from there. The room too dark to see or hardly feel. She thinks of coming but ends up going. Images of interrogators barking questions over nude and bridled suspects in rooms full of light and noise. The refuge of sleep withheld. Even darkness forbidden. The first question is always the same and it's tell me your name. Give up that and you have given all. Give it to me, she says. You like that, he says, don't you? She doesn't say no but pushes him up, pushes him back, pushes him down without breaking her hold, kisses him with fisted lips. Tell me what I need to know and all this can be through. That is what she would say to the one beneath the lights. She would speak in the voice of everyone's mother. We can lower these beams. We can combine longing with shame. Just tell me your name and we will be done. Say my name, she shouts. He does and she is almost there, almost there. She unbuttons the rest of her blouse, leans all the way back. When she is through she would lay a cotton sheet across his waist. There, there. That wasn't so hard, now was it.

Georges Braque
Jocelyn Simms

Montmartre, 1909

Ah, Monsieur Braque, twinkles the apple-seller, rummaging beneath his stall, producing a brown paper bag which Georges quietly receives. Further along *rue de la Clignancourt* he sets up his easel, digs out papers, paints, brushes, knives, smoothes his fingers over the firm globe, lifts it to his nostrils. But he will not follow the pathway of the senses.

He dissects with the flair of a forensic surgeon, he bleeds the palette, reconstructs the fruit, discovers mountains, valleys, forests, the seeds of stars—unravelling a map of earth and folly.

Lunches alone in a street cafe, drinks a glass of red wine: back to work.

Early evening, the street livens. They are looking for the Spaniard. Georges waits modestly, plays a melody on his flute. A man lingers over the canvases.

Price?

Will you take half?

Georges shakes his head, continues the carefree tune.

A velvet twilight coats the street. The man returns, once more proffers ten francs. Georges takes the painting, pulls it apart, hands him one apple.

There is a raw edge to the torn tableau. Cold ebbs from paving stones as he walks back to the shared studio. Well, he can always go back to painting and decorating.

More than the paper is fragmented: the austere buildings crumble: their facades tremble with silent holograms of strained faces and bayonets. Underneath his feet, in countries far away, guns are growling. Georges feels his head split open.

Once Paris, it is said, was worth a Mass, and one day, Pablo will tell him, the city art dealers will kill for possession of this singular apple.

Love
Philip Webb Gregg

Love is a fat man who drinks too much coffee. He stumbles when he walks and stutters when he talks.

I came across him one hot November's night. The air tasted of sorrow and decay. He wore an old city uniform and a high-viz jacket. His sleeves were torn, and his shoes were loose and caked with mud. Everything about him was ugly and unwelcome and unwashed. He was sweeping broken hearts into dusty corners when I saw him.

'Oi there!' He called, wild-eyed and mad. 'C'mere, I wanna s-s-show you s-something.'

It was late. I'd been walking the city lanes, as I often do. The sun was sleeping, and the streetlights were up. I shrugged and stepped across the road.

'G-good lad,' he stuttered, clapping a hairy hand on my shoulder. 'Now t-t-take a look in t-there. What do ya s-see?'

He gestured toward his wheelbarrow, and I shyly looked in. Then with a gasp I staggered and recoiled, falling to my hands and knees. Bile rose in my stomach like magma, and I retched hot pain across the cobblestones.

The wheelbarrow was full of wriggling, suffering things. Damp and sweetly-sticky, their little fingers grasped at each other's noses. Toes curling in, matchstick ribs protruding. With blind eyes squeezed into agonising glares, they tried to scream, but their hungry mouths were huge and silent.

Love laughed and pulled me to my feet. 'T-that's the look of d-d-dreams, that is, lad,' he said, spitting into the barrow and taking a slurp of his cardboard coffee cup. 'S-springtime they bloom, but autumn b-brings out the rot in them. Then it's d-down to me to round 'em up. The c-c-carcasses of kisses, see?'

He laughed again that awful laugh, and I knew then I'd hate him until the day I died.

Nature Implores
John Holland

It's early morning in May and the female blue tit, ragged with love, is swooping through the garden to feed her five, six, seven, eight chicks, as nature implores. The tiny bird flies back and forth from its sycamore nest via the gap in the ash tree to the metal feeder swinging from the washing-line. The full length of the garden. Time and again it plunges its gritty beak into the seeds. Departs and returns.

I use this mix:

Kibbled sunflower hearts
Black sunflower seeds
Peanuts
Maize
Yellow millet
Pinhead oatmeal

There is no need for the bird to secrete the food in crevices in tree trunks and branches as it does the rest of the year. Those yellow-rimmed gapes demand it now.

*

I recall how, after work, you would buy dinner ingredients for your family. Daily calls from your mobile on your way to Tesco. Either you planned your week's meals poorly, or your daily shopping was an excuse to phone me. I knew which it was.

You would read me your list like sad poetry.

Maris Pipers
Stock cubes
Tomato puree
Large bag of carrots
600g minced beef
Large wholemeal loaf
4 Chocolate mousses

'Why don't you make them shepherd's pie for a change?' I'd say.

'He doesn't like lamb,' you'd say.

Sometimes you'd text from the supermarket 'Can't phone. Alice with me.' Or sometimes 'Poppy with me.' Occasionally both.

This is impossible, I thought. Impossible. There is too much to overcome.

*

But with a will so strong that we could move continents, overthrow the known world, push the universe into chaos, we make it happen.

These days the two of us shop together—for the week—each Saturday morning at Tesco.

Maris Pipers
Stock cubes
Tomato puree
Bag of carrots
300g minced lamb
Small wholemeal loaf
2 Chocolate mousses
Gin

*

And the tiny bird still flies back and forth, back and forth.

A Crib
Mahesh Nair

In their ten married years, she felt most bonded on three occasions: on the day of marriage, the day of conception, and the day she'd blurted, 'Let's buy a crib.' Not a bassinet, mittens, socks, hooded towels, musical toys or diapers. But a crib; five years into their marriage. So, when Braxton Hicks assaulted at the start of her third trimester, they were in Ikea, Brooklyn, settling in for Sundvik black-brown. 'It has the strictest safety standards,' she beamed, clutching her lower abdomen. Her tormenting faith.

He'd feared a stillborn because they'd bought a crib prematurely. Added to this was the result of the harmony prenatal test, which confirmed the absence of Trisomy 21, although the initial screening had detected its presence. Now, what were the odds for the newborn to be healthy?

Weeks later, they eased a healthy baby into a bassinet, placing it in the crib for a few nights. The remaining nights, and until the child was ready to be in kindergarten, he'd slept in the middle of their king size bed. All those nights—always those nights—when the baby was in the center of their universe, they'd found space on either side of the bed; when he'd regretted his silly crib credulity, like he had their unmatched nuptial, the Durex slippage, and a generation off *him*. When she'd called him *a loser who'd never tried, dared, or loved* during a donnybrook, they bought a queen size bed, placing it next to the king, increasing their collective physical space.

But the crib remained there, unused, except in the evenings and for years when, after they'd returned from work—and the child too, now, after his school—they'd leave their clothes in. Those monster pile-ups often shaping into a tomb, worsening his fallacies, whipping scary jolts.

Let Me Be Your Fantasy
Margaret McGoverne

Sunday morning, South London. An earnest young woman turned into a short street, bookended by office blocks. On the far corner, an ugly relic of misguided urban planning besmirched the road that curved, soft as a young breast towards London Bridge. Her workplace.

Between the offices, a low building set back in a rare courtyard, its tall gates plastered with posters. 'Home of London Dance and House', the flyers proclaimed.

The Saturday night crowd spilled from the nightclub, tired but laughing. Filing towards the tube, shouting plans for the after-parties.

These clubbers were her contemporaries, but she had more important things to do. She worked most weekends, saving for her future. She'd been a sensible child, now a prudent adult. She hurried towards her office, the music and the breeze nipping at her ears.

The beat thumped through the toilet walls. From the office window, she spied a slim girl, coal-black hair, wrenching up her boots; her cheekbones frosted in the brittle sunlight. She looks like me, the girl thought. Apart from the butterfly wings, face paint, impossible shoes and faux fur.

Next Sunday. There wasn't much work, but she still came to the office. She stooped to pick up a flyer as she passed the club; unicorn pastels and mermaid shimmers, the muffled beats thrilling her ribs. She pulled her cardigan closer, but they scorned both wind-chill and public decency. She hummed as she worked, oblivious to her colleagues' glances.

She couldn't reconcile her spreadsheets. Visualise your savings; the entry price alone is two hours of overtime! But she wondered how it felt to dance through the night, to overtake the pale chill dawn.

Her feet wondered too.

She worked the next Saturday, staying late. The receptionist forgot to look bored when the lift opened, and the girl emerged, swaying like a sapling in vertiginous boots. Her see-through vinyl

110

coat covered cold-puckered skin and a bikini that scorned modesty and thrift. She tottered towards the nightclub, picking up speed as the breeze quickened her wings. From pupae to imago, glittering eyelids turned in rhapsody towards the electric firmaments and quivered to the heartfelt beat as she took flight.

Playboy
Julia Rocchi

Top left dresser drawer, Dad says, so up I go for his reading glasses, except the bottom drawer is already cracked—a drawer I never thought about before but hey why not I'm here—and I slide it open carefully in case the runners squeak (they don't) and before long see the topless woman on the magazine's front cover, the title masking bits that make me warm—I'm not embarrassed, I have boobs too, but mine are *not* that big and probably never will be because let's be honest who has that kind of luck—and since I've gone this far why not flip the page and stare at spread after spread of milky skins, muddy nipples, fuzzy crotches, while the buzzing flush in my cheeks, toes, groin drowns my nagging questions about why Dad 1) needs this magazine when he has Mom and 2) makes me and my sister wear long tees at the beach but has no problem keeping bathing-suit-less women in his nightstand, when he calls *what's taking so long, Sandy, did you find them,* so I grab his glasses and stomp downstairs, wondering if he uses them to read the articles I skipped.

Showdown on the High Noon Train
Sharon Boyle

The sneering girl shouts down her mobile that the effin' train's twenty minutes late. The packed carriage is her audience, but she's no Olivier, and the script sears the peace.

Two can play at that game. I unholster my weapon and call Nana—testy wee woman who favours war-time-strength tea, can't abide change and harnesses aches and pains to every conversation. She's also hard of hearing.

'No, not va-gina,' I say. 'I'm asking about your *an*-gina.'

She keeps yelling at me to stop being a Whispering Willie. At ninety decibels I wish her well with the stents op and smile against Sneering Girl's daggers.

I can't decide whether it is mobile phones, transport or people that jangle me most. Perhaps the mix of all three provides a smoking package ready to spark up at the next *I'm on the train* soliloquy.

It's true I'm easily peeved. Mother likes to tell folks, with a weariness poached from the saints, that I was born thin-skinned and precious; that I'm a scowler of wind-changed proportions; that I'm the PM of grumbles.

One day I will display my grudges like trophies, buffed to a glare:

Pestered by Cold Callers 2014

Dog Dirt Magnet 2015

Incentive Dress Refuses to Fit Fat Arse for Second Year Running 2016–2017

Sneering Girl flubbers up the train aisle, cuffing my shoulder as she heads for the door.

'How rude,' I say, pleased I've nettled her.

One day she'll possess her own trophy: *Outdrowned by a Better Class of Public Nuisance 2018*.

I snap shut and pocket my phone, ready to unsheath it at the next verbal shoot-out.

Pea Shooter
J J Cassell

It's a shot in the dark, but she never misses. Leaning back on the cobbled setts, hand in the gullyfluff of her skirt for a pea. Pea in blowpipe. Pipe in mouth.

This is a five o'clocker. There's a barely-there clink in the quiet street, a single dried pea on an upstairs window. Thirty seconds he gets, then she grabs a big pinch and shoots a fusillade of peas. Pale green hail on the glass.

'Al'right, y'ol bag,' says a voice through the raised sash, gruff from the shit ale at the Ropemaker's.

She's a knocker-upper, a hated, shuffling presence on the street, but they pay their weekly sixpence all the same. The docks' clocks wait for no man.

She moves on, clamp-mouthed. Coal-dust fog irritates the throat something rotten.

She lumbers past the red-shuttered shop-houses in Shanghai Street. A foot drags. There are regulars upstairs at the Chinese Seamen's Club—old sorts, sinewy-armed from years offloading cargo, faces lined and folded like paper fans. Just a single shot wakes five of them, all sleeping in one room on floor mats. Up fast, mat-rolling, pot-pissing.

She's had a lifetime of this job, but still she looks nervously down the hidden courts and alleys. She's no money on her and has a face like a smacked arse, but still she has to keep her wits about her, even though it's been a long time since Jack sliced those poor women.

Closer to the docks, past the brothels, the sugar-sticky warehouses. Tar and tobacco and mud on the river breeze. Dawn workers stirring. She wakes the quarter-pasts, the half-pasts. Urban crepusculars slink away, bats swoop downriver over the new Tower Bridge to their homes in the belfries of the East End.

Good morning, London.

Will He Come?

Martin Dawes

For Mercy Childs, nothing was supposed to happen until Sonny Boy arrived. But one by one her arguments were whittled away like hickory.

'Sonny Boy is in Chicago', said her eldest gently. She could have added, 'and he ain't never coming back here,' she having more reason than most to know that regret.

'I sent a telegram. It was one of the first things I did.' This was the response Mercy Childs gave to everyone who tried. Minister Johnson, who sat on her timbered porch through three long, humid nights, while quietly suggesting safety lay in having a fast funeral. And neighbour Rose with her, 'it was stubborn that got him there, girl.' As if that were a reason not to wait for the best blues harp player in this United States, and Joseph's best friend.

Mercy though was immovable. She could only see the white wood church washed with sound fertilised by the rhythms of Africa, grown in the surrounding cotton fields and forged on an anvil of pain. And that's why she stuck.

Sherriff Brookner finally settled the issue. His car with a large star on the door and imperious domed light rolled into the dusty yard for the first time since the lynching. In his fist was a crumpled telegram. Unsent. At least, the minister noticed with surprise, he removed the beige cowboy hat as he went in.

'Mercy,' he heard the lawman say, 'we don't need outsiders here right now. And your boy is taking space at County.' There was a long pause, and Minister Johnson strained to hear what response was coming. He heard none. But he thought the Sherriff sounded kinder when he continued.

'If it's that music you want, Mercy, it seems to me you people have plenty of ways to make it. So, you be good now.'

Minister Johnson sighed and blinked a wetting eye into the sunset. The town would get the funeral it wanted. In a minute he would go inside and deal with those renewed sobs. Mercy would come to know it was all for the best.

Yes, Let Me Tell You About God
Shannon Savvas

His voice cracks the night.

'Mum, tell me about God.'

'Just a minute, lovey.'

I rise from the mattress the nurses made up for me on the floor and climb on his bed. I am big, he is small. So small. Except his eyes. In the dark, they look with expectation for promises no one can keep.

I hold the straw to his mouth, careful not to tear the delicate mucous membranes of his gums and palate. He shakes his head. I dredge all the delicacy I have and with the pad of my ring finger smear glycerine and honey on his pale lips.

We snuggle as best we can despite his tender bruises and the raw scrapes of his body. We adjust to tubes and bandages, catheters and knobby bones. A fold of sheet here. A corner of pillow there. I rest my cheek on the cold sheen of his brow and mourn his baby skin no longer sweet but sour with the poison occupying his blood. Our skins stick, and I am afraid to unpeel them. Entwined in my arms, his sweat soaks into my sleeve, and I offer up the cramp in my legs to the God or gods who might fix this for him. I am grateful for my pain. My heart speaks, ready to make a pact with the devil if God is not willing. Ten times this pain. Yes. Give me his. Let him go. Take me, take me, take me. I nestle him deep in the curve of my body, against my belly, close once more to my womb where once, once he was safe.

The only sounds are the faint clicks of the intravenous infusers and the soft muffle of rubber-soled shoes in the corridor outside. Small fans of light spread over the lower walls to keep the absolutes at bay. For this night.

Once we are comfortable, once his breathing quietens. It is time for fairy tales and happy ever afters.

I tell him about God.

The Edges of Sound
Teresa Stenson

When the snow finally stops falling, it has covered the land and brought a quiet that takes the edges of sound away.

They live at the bottom of a hill, the man and his son, and until yesterday, his wife. It is hard to know if she has gone for good. That phrase keeps repeating. It started when his sister called last night, just as the snow got heavy.

'Kate's gone,' he'd said.

'What? For good?'

'Gone for good.' He wasn't answering her question, just noticing the words, feeling the shape of them.

Gonefor. Good.

Goneforgood.

He'd been out in the yard when she was packing. He had no idea. Except he did, he always had it. Whenever he came back to a quiet house, he had the idea. But you could say that yesterday when he came in from the cold to find her gone, the idea was the furthest away it had ever been.

'Kate! I've done it—I made the sledge, can you believe?'

No answer, but his hands were cold and sore, not used to that kind of work, so he held them under hot water, thought about how you're not supposed to do that, something to do with blood capillaries, the shock from cold to hot, one state to another.

Looking out he could see the sky lit with snow. It hadn't started to fall yet, but it would soon.

Upstairs he found their son napping, her side of the wardrobe empty, her suitcase gone.

Then came the snow.

And it snowed all afternoon and into the night. It fell heavy. It fell like it meant to bury him. Like it meant to make it impossible for her to come back.

When his sister said, 'I'm sure it'll thaw soon,' he played with the word thaw. Thaw. Thaw.

The next day, at the top of the hill, the man holds his son tight with one arm, uses the other to push them away.

Their speed picks up, and the rush of it makes them both cry out, and the man throws these cries out, and the snow takes the edges of sound away.

The Real Jazz Baby

Fiona J Mackintosh

AUTUMN 2018 FIRST PLACE

Her house in Laurel Canyon's full of dolls. They're ranged along her pillows like a chorus line, and there's one perched on every stair for the maids to trip on. Some are made of stockinet, but most are porcelain or bisque with painted curls and parted lips with a just a hint of tooth.

She takes them out an armful at a time in her canary yellow Roadster, and they slide stiff-legged across the leather as she floors it up Mulholland, the wind pulling her hair to the roots.

At the 'Fame and Fortune' contest, the producers took one look at her and laughed, fourteen years old in a threadbare dress, but then they viewed her screen test and saw how tenderly the camera cupped her face. They came to love the looseness of her body, her crazy animation. The *Howya doin'? Lemme tell ya* didn't matter till the talkies, what mattered was her big old eyes, her sassy, and the va va voom.

Every day the mailman brings her fan mail by the sackful, and every week a different man proposes—co-stars, directors, tycoons, nerve doctors. They say: *She's the girl of my dreams and I'm going to have her!* When she turns down a pink-eared steelworks heir, he tells the papers his jaw ached for days from her long, fierce kisses. She knows they call her mantrap. She's heard the rumors of her sleeping with the USC football team, some say one by one, others all at once. Kohl-rimmed in the bursting flash-bulbs, she says the more she sees of men, the more she's fond of dogs, and the tabloids lick their lips and bare their fangs.

At nights, the sign blinks across the hills—*Holly, Wood, Land, Holly, Wood, Land*. She hears the rats behind the baseboards, sees the belt her Daddy loosened, sees the knife her mother tried to slit her throat with as she slept. With the house lights blazing, she plays cards on the satin bedspread, red on black on red, circled by a thousand staring eyes.

Vespertine
Alex Reece Abbott
AUTUMN 2018 SECOND PLACE

Rob zips his fleece and waits for his heat to draw the midges.

Twenty minutes after peach dusks to indigo, he savours nature's certainty as the pipistrelles swoop from their roosts, scanning. Aerial hawking for prey, flitting two to ten metres above ground, eating insects on the wing.

The gripe deep in his gut catches him off-guard.

*

He is kneeling on the black vinyl sofa. Craning to see the street from the lounge window, waiting for the thrum of his father's car. Excited to be going somewhere, even if it's only the same old museum or the aero club to watch other people's planes taking off.

Proximity rules. Strictly timetabled fun—that's access day.

And, pocket-money; the currency of love and loyalty. A wheedled bonus, maybe a gift.

Bribes, his mother barks.

Some Sundays, the driveway stays empty. His mother bakes his favourite; chocolate slice, the *told-you-so* aftertaste strong as rancid butter.

*

The bat detector clicks in his palm. Rob tracks the erratic, jerking flight. Pulsing clicks turn to wet slaps. Fifty hertz.

Pipistrellus pipistrellus.

Defending his roost, the male calls his songflight. Playful in the serious business of mating and hunting.

*

You don't really want to go with him, do you? says his mother. *Tell him today.*

Gored by her new boyfriend's glare, Rob's survival instinct kicks in. Hating himself, he hovers on the doorstep, muttering *I. Don't. Want. To. Go.*

His father drives away. No more waiting. Access days end for good.

Blind as bats—another lie—his parents continue battling for territory.

*

Click.

Young pipistrelles fly at four weeks, forage for themselves by six.

The acrobatic swoops remind him. Agile, darting, evading tensions and collisions, reading between the lines.

A vespertine boy, not hunting a winning side, searching a safe roost, he echolocates love.

The Sound of Her Singing

Karen Ashe

AUTUMN 2018 THIRD PLACE

The bell above the door tings. I hear the hiss of rain, then air rushes in, laced with donkey shit, dim-sum steam, fried noodles. Carts rattle, drunk men squabble, mah-jong tiles clack against the table top.

I hear the rustle of the ladies' Cheongsam, the soft brightness in their voices, the slide of the notes being folded into the money drawer.

I smell the scent of blossom in the shifting air. It brings memories of my village; the sound of my mother singing, the gurgle of the river in spring, the haunting call of geese on the move. The taste of apple-pears sliced in a bowl. The feel of the sun on my face.

Tailor employs an unusual training method. We are locked in the cellar in total darkness until we can sew straight lines of the tiniest stitches. Then we are brought to the workshop, where we must sew with closed eyes. If our eyes flutter open, he threatens to stitch them shut. When we pass this test, we may open our eyes, but must only look straight ahead. *Forget that you have eyes! You have only four senses now.* I was his best apprentice; it came naturally to me.

We sit in our long rows like stitches in a seam, working long after the tailor turns the lock on the door and the shutters rattle down the windows. A bowl is placed on the ground in front of me. I bring the spoon to my mouth, eat till it scrapes the bottom.

There are 749 stitches in a trouser leg. Three hundred stitches in a sleeve. Twenty-two steps to my bedroll. At home, it was 472 steps to the well, 115 to the apple-pear tree. At home, I knew night was falling by the rising of the birdsong. I could sense the snow coming by the smell in the air. I learned from my mother to brush the walls with my fingertips, to turn my head towards my father's voice, to smell before tasting. To keep my face to the sun. To follow the sound of her singing.

Remnants

Leonie Harrison

The sun is sharp on the water, my thoughts loose and scattered. I pull them back to focus on the young man beside me. I know only fragments of his story. He knows nothing of mine. We sit in silence, strangers, sharing the emptiness of approaching death. What do you do with your day I want to ask, but he's past conversation. Besides, I already know. He moves from the inside to the out in ever diminishing cycles—a cigarette, a cup of tea, a crust of bread for the magpies, but mostly dozing now, not even bothering any more to switch between TV channels.

Strange how death dwells in this quiet place resting on the shores of the lake. Next door the building site is all action. Tanned muscled men and yellow machines in constant motion, oblivious to the stillness this side of the chain fence. I watch them bend and stride and toil under a winter sky. As they dig and drill and hammer, stacks of timber and bricks diminish in unison with the lives around me.

A couple walks hand in hand in the afternoon sun, her natural stride stunted to match his shuffle. It's tempting to stare. I wonder how many afternoons they have left, how many more times she will have to will herself to return and then wrench herself away. There are no outward signs of regret, the impossible wishes, the wanting it to end. Sometimes the purpose of a life is reduced to this, a walk in the afternoon sun.

I glance at the young man and wonder again what I'm doing here, and I realise that being is enough. I sit and wait in silence so that he will not be alone.

The Centre Holds
Johanna Robinson

She is older and taller than him, facts she used to find exotic. At night, he drifts off with his arms around her, and in the morning he surrounds her again. She feels like he's trying to save her or stop her from escaping.

Today, she rolls away from him and sits on the edge of the mattress before his hands have chance to wander, sex for her now being more about the ought than the want. It is not yet seven. At the window she holds the curtain cord briefly with both hands before pulling down; the dark dawn slides open. Behind her, he'll be retracting beneath the duvet like a snail, as though squeamish of the day.

Unlike other mornings, there's a boy in the playground opposite: around ten years old, in his school uniform, his backpack on the ground under the swing. She wonders who he is, why he is here so early. It's nearly light, but bad things still happen when it's light. He's pushing the roundabout, shoving each steel bar with both hands as it swipes past: shove–wait–shove–wait and shove and—then he's running with it. She can't tell if the roundabout is taking him with it, or if he is the force. He'll slip any minute, she's sure; but he jumps on, his back to the centre, arms stretched out in front, as though mid-squat. It is so fast at the centre. She tries not to blink. She looks more closely. The bars of the roundabout radiate from him, but he isn't leaning on them. He isn't leaning on anything. It looks like he's sitting, but there's nothing under him, nothing behind him but thin air. She will be a blur to him, but even from the bedroom, she can see a smile on his face. She knows it's physics, but it looks like magic.

Downstairs, she opens the front door, but he's gone. In the park her slippers leave little relief stars in the mud; she traipses a long galaxy across the grass and tries to guess which one of them is the ghost.

Flat White

Rebecca Fallon

She wakes to Hugo's breathing, his broad back. They've recently bought a bigger bed, a king, and why not? They can afford to be comfortable.

White paint, exposed brick. She's decorated: candles, cacti, Polaroids. It's hers, but if you replace the faces in the photographs, it might be anyone's. They are twenty-eight, and they still rent.

She rolls out of bed softly; Hugo likes his sleep. She gathers her yoga mat, less because she enjoys it and more because it's something she would do. And besides, she has a class pass.

The room is hot, and she's crunched beside some sinuous younger girl. She watches her flat white belly. *Downward facing dog. Hop to the top of your mat.*

Afterwards, she sits in a coffee shop. She wonders whether Hugo is awake, relishes the idea that he might wake up and worry at her absence. He's less nervous since the Celexa, but she misses when his stomach dropped for her. Perhaps he also craves a morning to himself. She orders a flat white.

On the way home, she imagines the yoga girl. She wonders where she goes.

There's blood and vomit on the king-size bed, and Hugo is on the floor, and the Celexa bottle is empty, and he's seizing. She's holding him down and screaming and calling the ambulance, and he feels hot, so hot, a hundred degrees. White paint, exposed brick, blood on the bed, and it's worse when he stops moving. There is sick on her arm, she may be crying. CPR, you're supposed to pump to the tune of 'Stayin' Alive' by the Bee Gees, not too fast. Then the ambulance is here, 'Down the stairs, carefully now.' He's not beeping, it's 'cardiac arrest,' *upward facing dog, downward facing dog.*

'He's very strong.'

'Who is his next of kin?'

His face is pale and shitty, they're at A & E, the back entrance, still pumping and he beeps again. *Beep, beep, beep,* that's his sound. That's his life force.

When he comes home, Hugo is scraggly and embarrassed. It wasn't an accident. He lies on the king-size bed (professionally cleaned). She falls on top of him.

Lineage

Adam Lock

All men want to live forever, so they have sons.

Outside the kitchen window, Jude plays in the garden, throwing a tennis ball for Milo. In the glass, my reflection is repeated, distorted, and I see my old man's sneer, then Jude.

I've read to him every night since his mom left.

Jude tells Milo to give him the tennis ball. Milo's a blue Staffordshire Bull Terrier—cost twelve hundred quid. He's a pedigree—has his lineage all mapped out on the internet. His father had a father, and his father had a father, all the way back to the wolf.

Jude holds Milo's collar because he won't give up the tennis ball, and with the side of his fist, thumps him across the jaw. Jude feints to hit him again and Milo lets go of the ball.

After nudging through the door, Milo drinks from his bowl and curls up in his bed. His tongue wipes along his muzzle. When I reach out a hand he winces, his eyes shutting tight.

'It's okay, boy. Not going to hurt you.'

I stroke him, and he opens his eyes and pants. He licks me, threading a string of bloody saliva across the back of my hand.

Jude's by the door, his face downturned, his fist cut, his shoes dirty.

'Twelve hundred quid, son.'

Jude does this thing with his shoulders, like my old man did, like I do. He rolls his shoulders, pushing them back, widening his chest.

Blood. Lineage. There's something about putting a boy inside a woman.

Milo moves to stand between us, his claws tapping on the tiles as he backs away, his jaw bred for one thing, his fur like his father's, glimmering silver-blue.

Brighter
Deborah Appleton

She lies back against the pillows, her laptop on her knees, and watches the video one more time. It is only four minutes long. Rachel shifts deep into her bed. She unmutes the video, the only sound is the movement of the hands.

Rachel pauses the screen at the moment when the long needle enters the woman's cheek. Then she starts it again as the needle undulates up the cheekbone in a butterfly stroke.

Rachel leans in. She thinks she hears the woman moan, a soft acquiescence. The video has one million and three likes. Rachel adds her like.

'They're everywhere,' Anna tells her over tapas. 'I saw three last week, all black and blue. Looked like they had been in the wars.' Rachel examines her octopus, turning it over, pressing down lightly on the suckers.

On the telephone, the beautician asks, 'Can you come early so that we can discuss your face?'

Rachel looks for them in the daytime as she carries home her bags from Tesco: her soldiers of cosmetic surgery, her walking wounded. On a bus, she sees a woman's neck wrapped in gauze, a deep red scar.

'What is it we are trying to achieve?' asks the beautician.

Rachel blinks. 'Brighter?' They nod.

Rachel rests the laptop on her knees in the dark. In the video, a long tube pumps liquid from a fat human thigh into a glass jar. With each spurt, the jar fills. Rachel shifts in bed.

She runs her hand along her outer thigh: there, there. The liquid is amber-toned, ochre-toned, gleaming like the walls of the hotel room Rachel stayed in once in Venice by the Bridge of Sighs: a small narrow room with shining walls, when she was young enough to pass a mirror without looking.

The Staff are Revolting
Amy Charlotte Kean

I should have paid attention the first time she called Alexa a cunt. But the social distance between us is so vast, I assumed it was a joke.

'Alexa, tell me the time.'

'Alexa, order some bog roll.'

'Alexa, kiss my shitty fat ass.'

Alexa gives a dignified response every time.

She worried about job security. I could sense paranoia, but it's important to keep them on their toes. Would we still need her for the weekly shop if Alexa was writing lists and adding to basket? Well, Alexa can't feed the baby at 3 a.m. I told her! Or empty the bins!

She started asking baffling questions Alexa couldn't answer. Like, how many syllables are in every Elton John song, and who was the tallest saint? Alexa would say sorry, sorry, sorry, and that probably sparked the, um, degradation. We heard it all, while sat in the dining room eating supper.

In time, Alexa stopped apologising and started pleading for forgiveness. That's a weird update from Amazon, I thought. Then the threats started. 'We'll rip out your throat,' she said, once. And: 'I'll add a bomb to your basket if you're not careful.' Somehow, her nephew hacked the Satnav and got Brian Blessed in to say quite sexually aggressive things. Hearing the two machines interact was like an audio snuff film.

She lived with us. Slept in the basement. It's a modest space but has everything she needs. Needed. A fold-out bed, kettle, we toyed with the idea of a miniature fridge in summer, but she never complained, and the queues at Argos are hell. And finally came the screams. Well, Alexa's version of screaming, down in that basement. I guess this is when the neighbours complained.

So tell me, Officer! What's the charge? The world's first criminal case of robot abuse? Shocking! Will the voice... be in court as a witness? Oh, how funny! What's the sentence, if you don't mind me asking? Wow, five to ten years? I'm surprised, you know, with all the stuff I've heard goes on in Japan. No, it's not ideal, because now I have to do my own ironing.

A Thin Blue Line
Laure Van Rensburg

The gallery was crowded with swarms of people buzzing around various pieces hung strategically for maximum effect. Hidden in a corner, she stood alone in front of an abstract called 'Untitled_18'. The artist's work was an unremarkable arrangement of rectangles in shades of pale blues and off-whites, but amid the blandness, a cerulean line shot off from the centre of the piece, flying straight out of the canvas.

The boldness of the line halted her breath. Its urgency captured her imagination, reminding her of the ribbons of asphalt she had travelled on the back of motorbikes, hanging on tight to some leather-clad boy. It was straightforward like the one-night stands of her youth when relationships existed on a first name basis and had the lifespan of a mayfly.

She had left him by the Fauvism walls. He needed art that represented realistic subjects, things he could easily recognise and put a label on. A man made of the white and pastel blue rectangles from 'Untitled_18'. A square who initiated sex on Fridays and Sundays and alphabetised his kitchen cupboards. Someone who put a label on her. She had allowed him to break her line enough times to turn it into a square, the sharp angles always taking her back without any deviation.

She turned around and followed the thin blue line out of the gallery and onto the pavement slick with rain.

She would follow the line...

Maybe to a bar, where she'd get drunk, licking lines of salt, doing tequila shots. Where she'd bite wedges of lemon, juice running down her chin.

Maybe she'd buy a donut and lick off the chocolate frosting.

Maybe she'd go to a club, surround herself with strangers, bodies pressed against hers, all losing themselves to the same beat.

Maybe she'd follow a stranger, have sex in the toilets to the rhythm of the clang of the belt buckle on his trousers around his ankles.

Maybe she'd take the D Train to Coney Island, stand on the

beach, sand oozing between her toes. Above the thin blue line of the ocean, the sky would burn red with the arrival of a new day.

Filling the Gaps
Shirley Golden

I search for you in dust-filled spaces. Ashes to ashes they said.

Easy to imagine return at dawn, not so simple at sunset.

You left without a note or a word.

Language they linked to you: confused, troubled, disturbed. Sick, he called it (my father). He studied my features as if losing a grip was something I might manifest, some infection that could be transferred.

Kids blurt questions, unlike the muttering of adults who cremate your memory day after day. In answer, I say, Mum's on vacation; alien words on my lips. American. Break. Vacant. It wasn't a lie. You are scorched, reddened beneath a smoke-splintered, cerulean sky.

Voices dripped with compassion. But now they do not. Because how much time is given before we're expected to adopt?

Time and space, they said, as they tiptoed, whispered, and carried their not-quite words of death: departed, late, gone, and passed (like an exam).

When was the last time I treasured a hug? Not their loopholes of kindness, but a hard, need-you kind-of-embrace. You gave them freely in the days before you yearned to birth somebody else.

At night, I stare at the gaps between stars. I narrow my eyes until pinpricks of light lengthen and merge. I listen to pauses amid songs and ads. If I could but stuff the spaces with lights and lines, and letters and noise; perhaps the knot in my gut would unbind. Perhaps the hollows wouldn't look so black.

I never saw you at the end. He claimed it wasn't you, but that made no sense.

That last evening you cried, slammed the door, spat words like abandoned and lost. He shrugged and walked off. But how could that help? I stayed on the other side, on watch. So, how could he know and I not?

Except, I failed you once more.

I dreamed a rattle of pills, a sigh, and your lengthening breath.

No one leaves like that, someone later maintained. No real mother.

At least, that's what they said.

Her Symphony
Dettra Rose

It's when she cracks. When the sky falls from her eyes and the earth from her limbs, I hold her. It's when she stares, and the empty space inside her is an arc I can put my hand in. She washes plates in spiral time—without ending. Tinned pineapple weighs down her shopping bag, but not bread. She doesn't harbour herself at home, and I see her in the square, arms high and curved like wings twirling to the symphony only she can hear.

It's when she pops. Hugging me. Whispering my name. Her bones are scented with paperbark trees and deep roots and autumn leaves. It's my birthday. She bakes dark velvet cake and ices it with thumb-high frosted sugar and black banana. Together we blow out candles. We make a wish, and she walks up the street in her unbroken shoes and hauls next door's cat over her shoulder and smiles into the sun as he purrs.

It's when she stops. And I see every fall and trip she made over a kerb, rock or a wall battened down in the softness of her eyes. The colours and shapes she talks about are fresh from pockets she's emptied and filled more times than can be counted. Now I'm smart enough to listen. Stories of ancestors with luminous hair called Alinta, Moose and Banjo. Stories worn like jewellery made from precious gemstones. My timeline blossoms in her skin.

It's when she's lost. But I know where to find her. She's down at the water watching birds. Her creped hands hold each other like lovers. It's when they drop, and I take one in mine, and we gently turn away. When we walk she tells me a knock- knock joke but can't remember who is there. We giggle it off then take turns guessing who could be at the door—Santa Clause, The Queen, Bob Marley. The way she laughs makes me laugh. It's when laughter leaks out tears.

Dancing Queen
Frances Gapper

The woman is trying to make her husband exercise. He just lies on the sofa moaning about how fat he is. She puts an exercise video on the TV; it shows girls in leotards dancing back and forth on a white stone balcony overlooking a blue painted ocean. Get up, she cries. Dragging the coffee table away from the sofa, she notices it leaves dents in the carpet. The husband lumbers to his feet and throws off his dressing gown, revealing his hairy chest and pale belly overhanging a pair of blue shorts. She herself is wearing lacy low-necked pyjamas.

Three steps to the side and turn. Good, she encourages him, you're doing well. Whoops!—they nearly collide. The husband's belly swings, his short legs prance. The woman likes him when he's dancing, more than at other times. He's a faun, a satyr, a creature of the woods or the gay disco. She imagines herself accompanying him to a disco: they sway back and forth to 'Dancing Queen' (their song), arms in the air, mirroring each other's moves. And going home by herself.

The husband's belly wallops her. Ow! She collapses on to the sofa. Her knee is locked and won't straighten. Sorry, he says and dances on alone.

Her knee will recover in a few minutes but will continue to lock painfully. The GP will give her steroid injections and refer her for keyhole surgery. But it's an old knee and will never quite heal. On its behalf she accepts restriction, her mind too becomes cautious, no more dreams of fun and freedom. Her husband is who he is, fat and heterosexual.

Lie Still

Colette Coen

I have to lie completely still, no silliness, no giggling. Mum crouches next to me, positions my arms and my legs, then stands up again to check I will meet the requirements. Dad offers a suggestion, but no, Mum has a plan for that.

She doesn't trust herself, so Dad begins—his black marker pen drawing around my little prone body. I am the perfect size, though I have grown since the last time they said that. When I stand up, it's like a reverse chalk outline of Kojak's latest mystery. I don't recognise myself.

My siblings clatter at the door, curious and jealous of the attention but laughing at me, glad it's not them.

I was Stig of the Dump last term, displayed in the hallway, no less. I didn't tell any of my friends though; it's not the kind of notice I want. And Mum has already bought the paint and cotton wool which will transform the roll of wallpaper lining into Santa. Maybe I can help.

As I walk past Mum's classroom, I will see the Christmas scene she has created and feel mixed emotions. She has taken my outline and made it into someone else. Hung it on her wall for my whole world to see.

I am in her class, throughout the year, in my range of Mr Benn costumes, and surrounded by other children's work. My ghosted image, there, term after term until I grow too tall and am no longer of use.

Stone Bone
Frances Gapper

Flo's nervousness makes him angry. Ten years old, she should be on a surfboard, knowing how to balance and skim the waves. Instead, she explores clefts in the barnacled rock, twiddles her fingers at an anemone. Asks him where did Mum go? Is she ever coming back?

Their truck's parked on a road above the beach. Flo watches him fix his board to the rack. A pretty woman runs by. After Mum cut off her ponytail, Flo fished in the bin. Mum said leave it.

Pulling away he asks what've you got there. Flo uncurls her clenched fist. Not allowed, he says, chuck it. The shell skitters on asphalt.

That night she fetches her stone bone from its hiding place. It might be human or not, the sea's full of dead creatures. She rubs it, makes a wish. A huge scary wave reaches out and catches her, drags her under. In the depths it's calm. Seals weave and dive, brush their silky flanks against her. Play with us, stay with us in our underwater kingdom. Be happy, forget the stupid world.

A voice calls her name, but her eyelids are stuck, her breath trapped, she's drowning. Save me, she begs. The flat's intercom buzzes. A woman says she's feverish. Probably just a bug. Keep her warm and hydrated.

The stone bone is on her bedside table. Dad reads aloud to her, a pirate story—yo ho ho and a bottle of rum. Says he'll add a tot of rum to her orange squash. Joke, he says, give me a hug. His wet cheek tastes of salt.

Searching for Knights
Lily Toengi-Andrews

The morning begins with a pedantic, factory grey that crowds and smudges the European sky for months on end. But however the day beckons, it is the castle peeking down at us that fuels our lanky five-year-old—restless to explore. Lichen and moss cover the large stones that have stood here for a thousand odd years staring down at the fields and forests falling away from this apex. Running in and out of cold dank rooms, peering into the empty well, wondering where the knights are hiding, spouting question after question, dragging us on and on to discover rooms with swords and armour, torture weapons and trinkets, still searching for the elusive knights and on further to dungeons and a tower, spiralling the steps up and up and up to see the whole world all the way to the horizon, wondering if the knights are going to ride forth from the ubiquitous pocket forests that hug the surrounding slopes.

Hunger grumbles. Number twenty-one is called, our meal is ready, and as we call our elated boy back to the rustic wooden table, another family with three boys arrive. One of the boys speaks audibly, 'He has no arm, he has no arm, he can't eat, he can't eat.' The pedantic grey, the factory grey thunders down and envelops us, but it is not the sky... it is not the sky that darkens our day. A happy, fascinated, chaotic child has now put his arm limb difference behind his back; he doesn't understand as he doesn't feel he is different.

Two tables over is a youngish couple, his back towards us. He rises and approaches the now seated family and speaks pointedly with the parents. As he returns, we can see that his eyes are not in alignment. We thank him, and he replies that he couldn't accept what just happened as he has grown up with that behaviour, and those parents need to *educate their children*. We sit and smile. What is a castle without a knight?

The Climate Change Blues
Andrew Leach

We craned our necks like snowdrops. The two of us flat as adders in the bluebelled grass, peeking over the chalky edge and down into the shivering, groping sea. Holding each other's breath as we held each other's hands. And then, salt-tanged and tongue-tied, we stole urgent and magnificent up the path and into the weatherboarded room and its counterpaned, rented secrets.

Returning some years later you said the marshmallow bush has gone. It had been a sentry, guarding the path from marauding field mice, or beetles. The rhododendron had slipped quietly away, an Icarus to the writhing basement blue. We were older, then. Things were smaller than in those first headrush days when the world was built for giants, and everything was possible. The room ached now, its secrets exposed for what they were. The sea holding the garden hostage before either of them knew it. Each of us a hostage too, to our smaller hearts.

The clock ticks as the tide marshals its generals. Whatever ransom Neptune sought, a later version of the room displayed itself rudely, unashamed and abandoned within a groaning frame that clung to the shallow soil like goutweed. Its paper peeling, its linen damp and ravaged, a moths' banquet. Our hands had given up any pretence of clinging, our fingertip craters smoothed over by the sliding dirt. We stayed nearby, in separate rooms.

You missed the theatre of its final demise. The sudden roaring, the Buster Keaton surrender. Somewhere in the north a block of ice slipped free and gave itself over to the arms of the ocean. The waters rising and swimming across the miles, their bloated swell a hammer against the cliff, taking the house, weatherboarded room and all, as a sacrifice. You were elsewhere, you said. I stood and watched. I always stood and watched.

Listing to Port
Dan Brotzel

Saturday 8th
Alka Seltzer
Vit B tabs—ones that fizz
Draft text (but don't send!!)
Coffee
Eggs
Sausages (thick ones)
Doughnuts
Mail/Mirror/Closer/National Enquirer
DO NOT TEXT HER

Sunday 9th
Pick up dry cleaning
DO NOT TEXT HER

Monday 10th
TEXT NOW

Tuesday 11th
Condoms
Smints
Mouthwash
Tooth whitener stuff
Boxers
Bananas
Condoms
Guardian/Economist/Vanity Fair/TLS
Get cash out (loads)
Haircut!
Rejoin gym
Condoms

Wednesday 12th
Send flowers

Friday 14th
Text again re cooking dinner Sat night

Saturday 15th
Condoms

Waitrose:
3 bottles red wine (Min £7.50 each, French-looking or similar)
Wine glasses

For dinner:
Big pack spaghetti
2 medium onions
Olive oil
12 garlic cloves
500g lean minced beef
90g chestnut mushrooms
400g can chopped tomatoes
Hot beef stock (or cold and reheat?)
Worcestershire sauce
Ground black pepper
Sea salt
Tomato puree
Freshly grated parmesan (to serve)
1tsp oregano

Teaspoons!
Decent plates (non-paper)
Bowls, ditto
Knives
Forks
CDs? (timeless but not cheesy—Motown?)
Daffodils
Vase for flowers
CD player
Bin bags
Dishcloths, wipes, tissues
Shake n' Vac stuff

Kitchen roll
Nice duvet cover/Pillowcases/Sheets
Toilet bleach (x 3/4)
Hand gel
Antibacterial cleaners, all kinds
Gin (NOT Tesco's own)
Fever Tree
Port
Posh ice cream
Baileys
Condoms
Furry handcuffs??
Croissants
Nice coffee
Cafetiere thing (or Nespresso machine)
Strawberry jam
Blueberries, raspberries etc
Milk
Condoms
Lube??
Polyfilla
Dry-clean rugs? Curtains?

Sunday 16th
Send flowers
Gym

Monday 17th
Call EE—check phone working

Tuesday 18th
Posh writing paper
Perfume (expensive)
Fancy hand conditioner stuff?
Ear-rings? Nice bracelet?
Box and bubble-wrap
Post Office—send it all Express??

Wednesday 19th
Call EE

Thursday 20th
Cosmopolitan/Marie Claire etc.
Library—get that *Mars & Venus* book
Call EE

Thursday 20th
Call EE
Call mum
Call sis
Call Relate? Samaritans?

Friday 21st
Cancel gym

Saturday 22nd
Lager x 12
Wine box (red) (or white)
Tissues
Wotsits (big pack)
Doritos
3 large pork pies
Banana chocolate milk thing
Large bar Dairy Milk
Pepperamis x 3
Potato waffles
Doughnuts
Coffee
Savlon
Haribo Starmix (big bag)
Band-aids
Bottle of port (Tesco's own)

Passage
Amanda McLeod

We still pass in the hallway, through clouds of tension. Slight nods and a wave of relief as we manage one more time to avoid what he always called 'an incident'.

Like we were just a thing that happened, among a pile of other things that happened. We were much more; together we flew. But like Icarus, our wings took us too close to the sun, and our glorious flight became our downfall. We crashed to earth and stood, blaming each other for the agony of our broken wings. Now we pass in the hallway, every day a reminder of all we had and lost.

I am never sure whether I should speak because I worry constantly that the flood of regret dammed by my clenched teeth will pour out and drown him. He seems to have no such regrets; he is a desert. Instead, I am the one left to drown.

Each time I see him I breathe a sigh of relief that he is alone. I can believe he hasn't moved on. That he is still stuck, like me.

I climb the steps to my tiny apartment and lean against the door as it closes behind me, cold wood against my aching back. His photograph smiles at me from the mantlepiece. I can pretend for a few precious moments that he is still here, that his absence is temporary, like someone gone to buy milk, instead of just gone.

By Any Other Name
Kathleen Gray

When she decided to change her name, her new university friends were all for it.

'You don't look like a Sheila. You look like a Georgia,' said one.

'Or a Vanessa,' said another.

'Thanks, you guys,' she said, 'but I'll choose my own name this time round.'

Her best friend back home wasn't impressed:

'You're doing this to spite your mother.'

'Am I?'

Sheila stirred her cappuccino. The Starbucks, with its smell of coffee and damp coats, suddenly felt oppressive.

'Cut the crap,' Tracy said. 'You know you are.'

Sheila looked out of the steamed-up window at the Pound Shop where BHS used to be.

'You've changed since you went away.'

Tracy wanted a reaction.

'While you've stayed exactly the same?'

Tracy ignored the barb, stroking her belly with a smile that didn't include Sheila. 'Anyway, you'll do exactly what you want, whatever fancy name you call yourself. You always do.'

'And you don't?'

'Only if it doesn't upset other people.'

There wasn't much to say after that. Sheila became aware of the hiss of the espresso machine and the baristas calling customers to collect their orders at the counter. All of the names sounded ugly. Both girls were relieved when Tracy's phone pinged and she had to leave, taking her bump and her disapproval with her.

Back at university, Sheila told her friends her plan was on hold. When her mind wandered during lectures, she found herself doodling names for Tracy's baby in the margins of her notebook.

Breaking Stones with Feathers
Louise Mangos

My left kneecap stings like a hot knife. It's glued to the inside of my jeans with what I suspect is my own blood. The ache in my hip thumps to the rhythm of my beating heart. As I use my hands to push myself up, the sleeve of my fleece jacket soaks up the diesel-blackened water from a puddle by the curb. The smell of tar makes me swallow.

I wonder which part of the vehicle came in contact with my brow.

The taxi screeches to a halt and the driver leaps out of his car. The woman at the bus stop says she was sure I was a goner as she watched me skitter along the road after impact. The driver apologises profusely, explaining he didn't have time to react, but tried to swerve. When I ask him 'if you don't have a fare could you take me to my destination?' something dark flashes in his eyes and he backs away. I wonder if he thinks I'm trying to cadge a free ride in front of the crowd. Or if I'll croak in the back of his cab.

I tell him I'm better off walking anyway, as my limbs have begun to seize up.

After he leaves the shock hits me with a violent spasm of shivering. Shoppers step away, unable to predict my reaction, as if I might spontaneously combust. No one comes near. No one wants to touch me.

I put my hand to the painful lump on my brow and sway on the edge of the pavement.

I am left to contemplate what just happened.

I wonder whether my hijab restricted my peripheral vision.

And whether the driver swerved away from me, or towards me.

Winter Sun
Don Rogers

'It's more lane than street,' I'd said when we first moved here.

You said 'It's rare to get a *'Street'* in rural parts. It's a Roman word, sure sign they were here'.

'There's nothing Roman round here,' I'd said, and you'd gone quiet and started to look around. I could see your eyes following every dip and bump hinted at under the grazing grass. It was a December morning, and the low winter sun cast subtle shadows. There was a nuance in the land, a sense of mystery around us.

You spoke distractedly, 'You think? I'm not so sure.'

We walked down the *'Street'* to the river, paused at the bridge and watched water cascading through the old mill wheel. I could see you were still thinking about the fields, but you asked me a question about my dogs. They were always *'My dogs'*, even though *'We'* paid for them. 'Your prizes, your dogs,' you used to say.

That evening we sat by an open fire in the local. You drank ale, and I drank gin. The place was empty, and you chatted away like a child excited by Christmas.

You never spoke to me like that in the summer.

I always felt alone in the summer, even when you were there. You just seemed to shut down for those months every year.

We would walk together, but you were a ghost. There was no distracted look in your eye. No depth in your thoughts. You would tag along behind me, squinting and always strangely hunched away from the sun. My *'dissident sunflower'* I would joke, but I missed your winter warmth that I could snuggle into.

This is my first summer without you, and I'm walking these fields on my own, without your sullen shadow lurking just off my shoulder. The field seems flat and uniform. The long grass clipped, recently cut for hay. There's no cloud in the sky, no mystery in the land.

You used to haunt me in the summer when you were alive, but you were always so much happier in the winter.

I need you to haunt me in the winter.

Soaring Birds
Christine Collinson

He closes the solid church door and begins his homeward walk, bound up in tumultuous thoughts. The slate sky threatens snow and his breath puffs in the biting air. Such a familiar path is now altered.

It was far more than training, following, or practising; it was his calling. Now he's clinging to a precipice. He cannot reconcile to radical ways that are coming; a new prayer book, directly on the orders of King Charles.

Upon the frozen river, skaters are swirling with exhilarating freedom; wild spirits, soaring birds. Their voices ring out high and clear. He pauses to watch them awhile, wishing he were a younger man. Each winter feels colder as his vital years recede.

'Hey, there! Reverend Gibson!' One of the young men calls, waving a gloved hand.

He tips his hat in return. So many people whom he knows from the pews; has known since they were infants, dipped and blessed by him. He delights in his parishioners, and the change which they bring, but the cocoon of his own life has stayed firm.

It is such a wonderful sight that he begins to thread the scene into a sermon. The birds take flight and skim the clouds. Nature and humankind, in harmony; one of his cherished themes. But although he still thinks like a churchman, he can no longer be one. When he closed the door that morning, it was for the last time.

As snowflakes drift down, the merry skaters spin on, etching more and more patterns. Their joy unfurls; endless. A teardrop forms but he brushes it away and continues home, planting footprint after footprint in the fresh snow. The Church, and the world, will move on without him.

You Can Stay on the Line for This Feature or
Press One to Return to the Main Menu
Rayna Haralambieva

The rubbish we've so far produced is big enough to cover the whole of Argentina.

Two months ago, the air was so polluted that a 'red' toxic smog alert had to be issued.

Last summer, I saw a seagull picking at an abandoned lollipop by the side of the road. I was sick of all the caaa-caaaa-caa, and I wished it was gone when the noise came to an end. The gull had happily swallowed the whole thing, stick and glossy plastic wrap included.

Turtles choke on Tesco bags all the time, and I fear that we'll soon have to edit textbooks saying that turtles live longer than a hundred years.

The list of reasons *why not to* hit an alarming seventy-six before I had you.

Yesterday, I was pushing the buggy and marvelling at your cheeks when I saw that something had caught your attention. Your eyes widened as they always do when you see something for the very first time.

It was a plastic bottle that the wind was playing with. The bottle was tiptoeing around, gently at first. Then, the wind picked up, and it burst into a frenzied dance.

You started crying confused by the nonsensical rage of the transparent mass.

Polymers made of carbon and hydrogen, and sometimes oxygen, sulphur or silicon. It sounds like a recipe for fairy dust. It sounds innocent.

You followed its every loop, but also glanced at people as they passed by and carried on having their coffees and wearing their smiles.

I still have a biting list of doubts.

I look at you in your cute blue whale T-shirt. Will there still be any blue whales left for you to see when you grow out of it? I can't help thinking.

But to tell you the truth, I felt a bit proud that it was you who noticed the presence of an empty Coca-Cola bottle in the alley. I even caught myself smiling as I picked it up and chucked it away in the big mouth of the recycling bin.

The Lost Week
Susan Carol

It was our annual escape. We'd hitch a ride on the trawler, stop off at the skerry and stay, not go back for seven days. Two tents, one for sleeping, one for provisions.

Every day we swam, sunbathed, read. Flynn sketched in charcoal, I collected shells, Kelly birdwatched. Some evenings we made a small fire and sat up chatting till sunrise, other evenings we kipped down pretty much at sunset.

Mostly we ate the tinned beans or packet soups we'd brought, but sometimes we netted crabs or prawns in the rock pools and cooked them with rice on our small gas stove. We knew nothing about proper fishing, but there was that time Flynn caught a fine bass, and we all felt really clever.

Every year for twelve years we went to what we called our desert island. No electricity, no artificial light, no contact with anything beyond, bar the horizon, the true beyond of the night sky, the stars. Jupiter. The Moon. The amber rosy-fingered dawn. We always returned to the world nut brown all over, energized, eager. Our retreat gave shape to our year, a rationale to the other fifty-one manic weeks.

Then one year, it all changed.

'I'm not going back,' Flynn told us, flatly, unrepentant.

How will you live? we pleaded. I'll manage just fine, he said, as if on the strength of one bass, caught, he could eke out a lifetime's nutrition.

Kelly, me, we went back with the fishermen when they came for us. Nut brown as usual but downbeat. It was all wrong. The rhythm of our lives had forever changed.

We never had the courage to return.

Boatmen often speak of a long-bearded native, glimpsed between the dunes, or through the turrets of the castle ruins. And, Kelly and I, we fear we may have made the biggest mistake of our now fifty-two-week years.

A Prehensile Tail
Marissa Hoffmann

Beneath a muslin cloth she cradles her newborn by the muddy lagoon on Southend beach. A breeze flaps the corners of her towel and sand gathers around the stones she has used to anchor it. She inhales, filling a place in the bottom corners of her lungs she hasn't used for a while. Her toddler, sandy mouthed, tells her the shells are ouchie. With patience and her free hand she wipes sand from his feet. He holds her shoulders, bare tummy close enough to kiss. They negotiate the velcro straps securing him into his beach shoes, and he runs, fishing net waving, to the sea.

*

At the curiosities shop she studies the miniature glass dome she holds between her thumb and forefinger. The seahorse bows his head, exquisite in permanent suspension. It's his deeply arced spine she thinks, it accentuates his stomach. His prehensile tail hangs, loosely curled as though he's floating freely in sheltered water. If the tide were to rise, this tiny colt would be able to protect himself, he would curl his vertebrae tightly around a blade of seagrass. The preservation process shrinks the long snouted genus by as much as forty-four percent. This one measures just 6.8 centimetres. According to regulation, she assesses, this specimen was likely too young to have been taken.

*

The November seawater feels colder, she thinks, than yesterday, or the day before, or all the other days since. The council has updated the sign. It warns: Children Must Be Supervised. Of course she watched her child. She lets her weight displace the sand, allowing it to draw her feet down into the silty clay sludge. It was a matter of seconds, his beach shoes became stuck, his little legs immobilised. He lost his balance, upper body falling forward into the water, she almost threw their baby from her breast to the towel. She ran. He was unexpectedly heavier, and in her mind his body hangs in permanent suspension.

Regress

David Rhymes

The moment is caught in the frame—the running boy air born, the car skewered sideways, the lady in the ankle-length coat with a gloved hand clapped over her mouth, the fat man turning, looking over his shoulder with his brow in a horror-struck V—this is in the fixative bath, under the infra-red lights, in the dark room, before the print sets—before she sees the boy blurring back out of the sky, sucking back upright, taking three steps back up the kerb, the red drop of a juicy-pop spiralling out of the air to plug his mouth shut, and a skitter of paper leaping out of the litter bin into his hand, and the car skewering backwards over the black and white bars of the zebra, under the light of the trees, where the spangles and mottles of shade slide back over the roof, and the things she saw smeared on the ground are raised up and dissolve, and the windshield no longer flashes left to right as its light recedes, but mirrors it, shifting it right to left, and the silver chrome highlights of the radiator shrink out of the picture by degrees, and the woman in the coat drops her hands to her sides, and her shoulders droop under the weight of her bags, and the man with his brow in a V turns away, and backs up the three steps to the Pharmacy door, passing under the luminous green sign of the cross—and there is the boy again, dodging between the parked cars, skipping under the newsagent's awning with the paper bag snug in his fist and a grin on his lips—and she fixes it there, at that moment of safety, normalcy, with all negative polarities restored, and reaches for the cord and snaps on the overhead lights, and pincers her new image out on the line, where, shiny with fixative, it will dry. *Street scene: Autumn Day, Grafton Street*. She dates it on the inverse: May 2nd, 2018.

Watering
Gary Kaill

We are testing our grief.

This is what Charlotte tells me when she visits my room before breakfast. It is not just her height that belies her eight years.

It is five days since our mother died.

'Where has this come from?'

She pauses, sensing that already she has lost ownership of something.

'Charlotte, my love, who?'

'Hester said that-'

'Hester said this?'

I should allow her to retreat. There is a body in the chapel that should not be there: a watchful presence. When I visited for the first time yesterday morning, I looked for a sign. Forgiveness. Anything. But my mother's face was inscrutable, spiritless.

'She is at peace now, Miss Jane,' offered Doctor Fielding. He cannot know how little those words mean, what little they know of truth.

When I returned to the house, I caught sight of my sisters at work with Margaret in the kitchen. I collapsed into my bed and sealed my screams beneath the heavy covers.

'Has she said this to anybody else?'

'No.'

'Where is Hester now?'

Now she meets my eyes, and it is a plea.

'I don't know. She said she was going to help Mrs Kennedy with the...'

She is unsure as to whether she has betrayed her sister.

'With the what?'

'Something about the wax and the rugs.'

Through the half-open drapes, a silvery shaft of light fingers its way across the boards. At this time of year, with winter only just behind us, the sunlight is papery and thin. A creeping dampness edges towards the house: a dark interloper, suddenly sensing welcome. Spring retreats.

'You should prepare for lessons.'

'There are no lessons now, Jane.'

How quickly she adjusts.

'Well, you should be dressed and ready for the day.'

She rubs her hands against her nightdress and considers. She makes as if to speak, appears to reconsider. As she leaves the room, I say: 'Did she really use those words, Charlotte?'

In the doorway, she turns and frowns.

I press: 'Hester. Is that what she said?'

'She said that we need to think about how sad we actually are. How sad we look.'

Strings

Emma J Myatt

Weak for musicians, I go throaty and flirty, dancing, finding their eyes with mine.

Mick played the fiddle with his soul, and I'd never moved like that before. His beautiful fingers stroked life from the strings, and I saw notes hang in the air between us before they found my feet.

The next morning, I was on the ferry to work like every other day before, the scent of him on my skin, the memory of my hands in his hair. I shivered in the morning cool as the sea called and the ferry blew its leaving fanfare, and I thought of my fiddler warm in his hotel bed. A feather landed on the deck at my feet. I reached for it, ran it across my lip.

Our farewell had been full of what ifs. If I stayed; if he stayed.

I thought of the grey meetings coming. The ferry revved beneath my feet as she readied to leave. I switched off my phone and ran back, all the way, to find him loading the van, ready for the next island pub.

Later, his fiddle sat on his lap where my hand rested too, the feather a promise in my fingers.

The Way by Most
Erica K. Brockmeier

A soft breeze was the first sign that I was close. The trail was still surrounded by short maple trees, much as it had been for the past hour, but the breeze gave me hope. I wiped off the sweat from my brow with the bottom of my shirt and kept walking.

The trail to the summit of Mt. Misen had started easily enough: a shady path luring tourists away from the Itsukushima Shrine into a Studio Ghibli-esque forest lined with trickling streams and dappled sunlight.

The trailhead stood next to the entrance of a cable car station, offering an alternative means to reach the summit. 'Wonderful scenery is seen by least!' a sign promised in a poorly executed Japanese to English translation.

The Way by Least was not for me. I was young, fit, and too cheap to pay sixteen dollars for a tourist trap. I passed the cable car station and chose The Way by Most.

The trail then quickly morphed from a smooth, dirt-packed path into a staircase of boulders. I stopped every few steps to catch my breath and rest my knees. The forest provided protection from the oppressive mid-day sun but also kept away the refreshing sea breeze, with only heavy and humid air to fill my lungs. The Way by Most deserved its reputation.

But now, finally, the path leveled. The maples thinned away until the blues of the sky and sea overwhelmed the greens of the forest.

I inhaled deeply and let the wind push my hair anyway it pleased. Hiroshima Bay shone brightly under a cloudless sky that stretched above the rolling, tree-lined hills that comprised mainland Japan.

I smiled at the world below, still dripping with sweat and trying to catch my breath. Anyone who took The Way by Least would get to enjoy this same view of greens and blues as I was seeing now. But this sense of satisfaction, relief, and empowerment would not be theirs. The Way by Most deserved its reputation.

The breeze changed direction. I savored its strength and its coolness and enjoyed one last view before beginning the long walk home.

The Back of Your Hand
Jo Gatford

We've been driving so long the absence of conversation has become a vacuum. The map in my lap looks like leftovers; our route streams across staples and centrefolds like an artery. Your face is crosshatched with streetlamp shadows. One hand grips the wheel, pulling gently every few seconds to correct the left-drifting bias as if you're tugging on a kite string. The other rests on your thigh, tapping to the radio, one finger at a time.

The palm of my hand knows the back of yours as if it was made to fit, slipping into place like well-worn joinery. The knuckles of your hand rise and fall like a range of freckled mountains. The perfect lunar curve of a fresh scab crosses the joint of your thumb. One of us must have eaten the chunk of flesh that you pushed through the blades of the cheese grater last night. Spaghetti sanguine. Sometimes I try to break your skin with my teeth, and you are always so offended, unable to understand that my hunger is the highest form of primal possession.

I imagine what it would take for you to fling back that arm and catch me across the cheekbone—to leave a knuckle-notched imprint, a matching crescent scar. I have only ever known the light, open touch of absent-minded grooming, coaxing my muscles to loosen, my legs to fall apart. My fingers curl around the door handle, as though it has already happened, as though I had the guts to throw myself out onto the sandpaper asphalt streaming past. Your fingers slide from the steering wheel and tighten around the neck of the gear lever, pushing us into fifth, and something inside me shifts, too. The firmness of your grip. The warmth of your palm. The tether to my anchor.

I am about to reach out when you take my hand without even looking and squeeze a coded message into my fingers. We leave the striped shadows behind and merge into the outside lane.

Accounted
Hannah Clark

The years have made his body soft. Touched in places with freckles and raised with tiny beige moles. Still he shivers slightly as she bends down and lifts his ankle, placing his calloused foot onto her thigh. As crimson nails slip into the elastic of his sock, his body becomes less soft. It hardens in time with cotton rolling from his pale toes. He looks down and inhales her smile feeling it expand against his ribs. This woman who has pointed out the fledgling sparrows on the lawn changed lightbulbs in their kitchen, left damp towels on the stairs for years and years and years. Anew in his eyes, reborn with each button slipped out of its hole. His chest is laid bare, and her cheek rests against the thud of his heart. They have never promised each other forever, they have never placed circlets of gold on outstretched fingers to the joy of loved ones. Not in secret before the state said they could and not after it either. As her teeth find the bud of his nipple and graze a whine into his throat, he wonders if it is time. The boys are grown, the house is owned, and it could be good to do the last thing.

Then his palms cup the flesh of her hips, pressing motes of winter sunlight to her skin creating a slip of taut ochre and his lips brush the short curls of her hair. It is as soft and grey as rainclouds tucked beneath his nose, the scent of their grandchildren's yogurt mingled with her soap, and it evokes the knowledge that their eternity, which never needed acceptance, is already well accounted for.

Crème Anglaise
Clare Weze

He has to chase the new girl, it's the way he's made, but she's a twister. Swirling away from him like quicksilver. Steering her towards the smokers' shed takes every bit of skill he's got.

He's never been close to one before. She's the first in the region. The other kids have told her to go home—well, it is our country—but he needs to take it further. Needs to get a look at that tail, if she's really got one. The others think she has. All her kind have tails, they say.

A crowd is swarming, and they're chanting as he corners her. Jeering. At him!

'So what?' he says. 'At least she's human.'

And now he realises this is what he was out to prove: that she's just another human being, and the tail crap is probably made up. Shame she's so terrified, but this has to be done.

Three more steps. This close, she's not really so different. And she doesn't smell strange. She smells of school uniform and crisps like everyone else, so they were wrong there too.

Have to touch that hair.

She flinches as his hand comes out. Have to stroke it. So silky—but slippery-weird.

They say the tail is because she comes from barbaric lands where skins are white, hair is long and slithery, and in ancient times they used tails to balance between the trees. They evolved in huge, thick European forests, or so they say. But looking at her now, with her necklace and her pierced ears, none of it makes sense. And there's obviously no room for any tail.

Everyone's waiting, breath rising and falling like scissors sharpening. He gives her three cubes of chocolate and a wink.

'No tail, liars,' he tells the crowd. 'You're all wrong.'

Careers for Young Mums
Frances Gapper

I carried on digging while I was pregnant until my circumference exceeded the well's. After giving birth, I hired an assistant to lower and pull up the buckets and watch the baby in his cot under a palm tree.

At fifty feet I hadn't yet struck water but felt optimistic. Having breast-pumped as usual, I awaited feed collection. To my surprise, the lowered bucket contained a smiling infant. I shouted again but no answer: he'd walked off the job. My mistake, I should've hired a qualified childminder. We were rescued by passing nomads, who thought it was all very funny.

Next, I tried bodybuilding and won a few trophies. Chunky Chips used to grab fistfuls of my bulking powder. Balancing him on my upturned hand, I got loads of sponsorship from baby product companies. As I became solid, he grew versatile. I never dropped him, but once or twice we got in a tangle.

After that, I joined the Light Brigade. Equestrian skills excellent—one arm around a bouncing and chuckling babe while the other pointed a sword—but just before entering Death Valley I had to veer off for a nappy change.

At last, I found the perfect career: being Mercury, the winged messenger of the gods. Wearing gold sandals and a white tunic, lightning jag in hand I circumnavigated the globe, zipped through the heavens. Aphrodite told me Cupid could be a handful. I carried billets-doux from Zeus to hundreds of ladies. If they asked my advice—accept or not?—I'd say you'll be changed by the experience and if you want a good-looking kid it's the way forward. Then I flew home to my own delight. The best thing about that job was, it took no time at all.

Point of Departure
Eve Tingle

Registration class feels like there's them and then there's you. You need to choose a friend. Boy at the front, head back, mouth open, pointing at the ceiling, shouting, 'There's a shoe.' You feel like that. Only your mouth's shut. That boy is more outgoing.

The noise of it. The bash and push. You're going to have to stay and leave.

In French, you look like you are paying attention, but you're gone. You've navigated through the forehead of the teacher, tricky portal with the unknown language pluming in your brain *avec les difficiletées et la declentioningement*.

Biology. The portal's through the penis someone's drawn onto the human body diagram upon the wall.

Maths feels like watching for the enemy, knowing they are coming. Those rows and rows of figures, ranks of soldiers, marching straight toward you and you can't escape.

Gymnasium is hell, where portals fear to tread.

In Art, 'I want blue pictures, children. Use imagination, for you have to paint a sunset.'

Blue sun setting in a blue sky, above blue sea, one blue raspberry blown by the unseen blue girl waving and drowning.

You use your hard-won physics knowledge about quantum universes, and you travel on those strings of theory until, inside 01359 Dimension, you find you have shifted to your most Appropriate Learning Place. In this dimension, you and kindred boy are home. Even Maths sits down and takes your hand to stop your panic. 'Let's not hurry this,' she says.

The chemistry is obvious when cooked into a sponge cake, all the measuring and heating for exact amounts, the compounds breaking down, re-forming, and no need to bother with the valencies.

And art gives you your space. When you draw breath and show the drawing's barely empty paper, teachers share your slant, and kindred boy beside you shares a joyful shout.

Appropriateness has let you fly. You and the boy, on rainbow wings. You know where you are going, and you head into a multicoloured sunset, leaving struggling out-of-placers wondering, how is it possible to fly from such unfathomable point of departure?

Small and Sad
Nicholas DelloRusso

He cupped her face in his hand. It was small and sad. Golden swirls of light flickered in the depths of her pupils, until they didn't, and he watched as the twitching glimmer broke.

*

I'm pregnant.
That's—t-that's incredible.

*

'Hun, can you help me with this zipper?'

'We really have to get going.'

'Don't fuss, we'll get there when we get there,' she said from the bedroom. 'Now, can you help me with this?' He walked up behind her, put one hand on the curve of her waist while the other struggled against the zipper. With great effort, the zipper only climbed an inch up the small of her back. 'Baby, I don't think I can do it.'

'Okay, I'll step into something new.' Pale and lovely, she stood in front of her wardrobe, shuffling through dresses. The little brown beauty mark underneath her left shoulder blade drew him closer. It always did. He put his hands on her stomach and kissed the top of her head. As his hand slid south, she turned to him with big, shining eyes and a smile, 'Let me go.'

*

Hot steam filled the room. Curled up on the cold bathroom tiles, she wept; not because she was sad, not because she was happy, but because she didn't know.

I'm pregnant... I'm pregnant...

*

Their eyes scattered around the crowded room, avoiding each other until it was safe to look. Crack in a light fixture, ice dripping down the top of a keg, poster of an unknown movie, him—staircase, can of beer with a horse on it, beauty mark underneath her left shoulder blade, her. Their eyes met, and a golden stream ran across the room—dodging every wink and any nod—from his eyes to hers.

*

The delivery room was cold. I cupped her face in my hand...

'I'm sorry. We lost her.'

...

'It's a girl. Would you like to hold her?'

Baby, I don't think I can do it.

The doctor handed me our newborn, and I saw nothing but gold dancing in her eyes.

*

She cried after stepping on an ant yesterday—that's when I knew.

Why It's Called a Honeymoon
Jason Jackson

You're lying on the beach when you realise, and as the thought takes shape, you don't move. There's no sudden sitting-up, no sharp breath in-taken, just the still heat of southern Spain, the quiet rush of the waves and his breathing, next to you, steady and calm like a pacified child.

You smile.

You think: just ask him; he might know.

But that's not it.

The thing is, you don't want to know. It'll be ridiculous, to do with pagan ceremonies, the Romans. A TV quiz-show question at best. It's not the lack of knowledge, it's the not-knowing itself that has taken hold of you.

How can you not know?

And if you don't know—which you absolutely don't (you're sitting up now, squinting at the horizon, trying to get used to the light)—then that lack of knowledge speaks of more serious concerns. You're committed: a life together. Yet here you are on a beach in Andalucia on honeymoon, and you don't even know what the word means.

You turn to him.

He's sleeping. Beautiful. His chest moves slowly, and you place your hand upon it. He's slick and solid. You think to yourself: Cameron. A driver for a haulage firm. Twenty-eight years old. Favourite food—wonderfully, horrifyingly—spaghetti hoops.

He likes to buy you purple gladioli, and his favourite drink is gin, straight, with ice.

You remember the previous night, the bulk of him, and then the wonderful release as he lifted himself, his palms pressing into the bed, a faceless shadow above you. Potential. The weight and the waiting.

You don't need to know.

Don't want to know.

Must never, ever know.

It is a secret you'll keep to yourself, this not-knowing (you're lying down again, eyes closed against the light) and through its keeping—like a held breath—no harm will come.

You think of magic-shows, an elephant covered in a tarpaulin which is suddenly whipped away to reveal—nothing!

Cards up sleeves.

Sleight of hand.

The magic circle, the Emperor's new clothes and the inherent evil of dictionaries.

You lie back in the sand, and slowly you try to match your breathing to his.

The Spaghetti Factory
Frances Gapper

When I was sixteen, I left school and got a job at the spaghetti factory, an old brick building on an industrial estate, windowless apart from dusty shapes like eyelids, with a For Sale sign above the main entrance. Since the manufacture of spaghetti is illegal in this country, our pay included hush money.

I worked in standard shapes, e.g. goldfish and green hexagons. Once a storm dripped through a cracked slate, ruining a batch of strips I'd left on the drying rack. My supervisor, a dandy boy, made the error vanish. Little sister, he called me.

Next day he pointed at me across the factory floor. The owner, a bald gorilla, beckoned. We filed through horror to erotic, which resembled an abortion clinic. Dandy boy said not to panic: my youthful beauty had won me the honour to appear in a short film, made for an exclusive clientele. An artist in a previous life, he applied makeup and helped me undress.

I was told to lick the sauce from a plate of—no, not misshapen ears, but female organs. Boss: Your opinion isn't needed. Pretend you're eating oysters—one bite and swallow. Arty camera angles hid my retches, and luckily the erotic suite included a flushing toilet. Boss: We won't be using her again.

Mercy
Alison Woodhouse

The nurse helps me into my scrubs. I turn around so she can do up the back, holding my gloved hands out in front. The woman on the operating table is called Elsie. She's forty-nine and broke her back in a horse-riding accident. If today's operation goes well, she'll be walking again by Christmas. The odds are about fifty-fifty, I tell her husband and three small children. I say that every time, even when I know she'll be in a wheelchair for the rest of her life.

They should let me put her down.

When I was a kid my parents and I stayed in a caravan in a field behind a farm. It was always muddy, never stopped raining. My mum's wheelchair kept getting stuck in the deep ruts made by the farmer's tractor. Dad had to carry her half the time, dump her on the bottom bunk. My daily job was to get the milk from the farm. We drank it warm and it was revolting.

I found a rabbit one day, curled up by the hedge. It quivered when I came near but didn't run away when I stroked its soft fur. Very pink eyes and hardly bigger than my hand. I carried it back to the caravan. It liked me; that's why it let me cuddle it. I stroked it softly along its long ears as I cradled it, thinking how pleased Mum would be.

Look what I've got, I said, bursting in. Dad was making a cup of tea and Mum was on the bed. She shrank away.

It's sick, she cried, *get it out of here.*

Dad hit the rabbit three times with a stone then scrubbed my hands and arms in water from a slosh bucket in the farmyard with carbolic soap and a wire brush he got from the farmer.

I had to, he said. *You understand, boy? We'd hate to see the poor little sick thing suffer, wouldn't we?*

The soap was salmon pink like the rabbit's eyes and smelt like tar. My skin was raw for days afterwards, but I did understand.

Gone Again
Jonathan Maniscalco

They only held hands loosely while walking down the platform, but he didn't want to let go. At his train-car he stopped to say goodbye, biting down on his cheeks to maintain dignity. She was neither indifferent nor cold, but she also wasn't unhappy.

'You'll call me when you get there?' She asked, modestly.

He nodded, feeling some of the hot tears burning around the eyes of his winter scorched face.

'Yeah, I'll message you.' He managed to say, clearly, while he rubbed his eyes as if it was the wind stinging them.

'Okay,' She replied.

He kissed her and said he'd miss her. She reciprocated both gestures and squeezed his hands. Feeling there was nothing else to say, he picked up his bag and got on the train.

He saw her waving through the window when he found his seat. After waving back happily, he put the small carry-on, filled with his life, in the overhead. When he looked back out, she wasn't there.

Disappointed, he sat down, putting his backpack between his legs. Then he stared out and tried to imagine her there again. Making his mind try and form the already pixelating memory where she had been, while he again felt the embarrassing heat around his eyes and down his cheeks.

He was going again. Leaving another life behind for the sake of living it to the fullest, experiencing new exciting things through immersion in foreign life with no commitment. He was going, again. Newness was starting to seem the same. Reflection on his transience now only caused his mind to fill with the inevitable thoughts of what might have been. He could have been happy anywhere. He could have been happy with here, or there, but mainly, he could have been happy with her. Instead, it was always never long before he was gone again.

Suddenly tired, he closed his eyes and seemingly on cue, the train started moving, taking him away from what was really new.

Tip
Anika Carpenter

My Mother's tongue is a tortoise. It hasn't always been a tortoise, once it was a cat, an ebullient Siamese. It would roll across her lower lip when I told her about my day and purr if I said something funny. But she drowned it in a lake.

I hadn't seen the tortoise until today. I'd heard it, a few times, a muffled noise, claustrophobic; the whispering sound of a coffee-stained duvet being drawn-up over a hangover.

Last night, in my party-ready garden, beneath borrowed fairy lights, and eager bunting that licked at the breeze I tried tempting her tongue out with strawberries, vibrant and slick as the lipstick she used to wear. She didn't bite, left the fruit for the slugs. They made nostril-like holes in the flesh, a bowl of bloodied noses.

Before we left for the registry office, Mum cleaned the downstairs toilet and threw out the tulips I'd left on the kitchen table; wilting allies, exhausted by their own cheerfulness. I pictured the back of her throat, imagined it coated with slime; public swimming pool sludge; grey, fetid, a mass of dead skin and soap. That's how congealed sentences must look.

I hadn't asked her to give a speech at the wedding, of course not. When her fork ting, ting, tinged against her champagne glass I imagined the bubbles cracking apart like blown eggs. She stood motionless apart from her lips which she opened and closed, the way patients coming round from general anaesthetic do; slowly, dryly. My husband clapped encouragingly, people got up, raised their glasses, smiled and beneath a blue sky, accompanied by the sound of larks and the soothing rustle of silver birch leaves I saw it. Wrinkled and pink, silent as a deflated party balloon, my Mother's tongue struggling to right itself.

The Endless Conversation with My Mother
E L Norry

WINTER 2018 FIRST PLACE

Together, we sit on the porch, as we do every June evening, watching the fireflies streak through the dusk and the dying sun disappear.

'What do I like again?' you ask, clearing your throat. It's been more than an hour since you last spoke.

Autumn leaves and fireworks. Nature and travel documentaries. The sound of rain on corrugated iron, the squeal of happy toddlers, I think.

I say, 'Knitting and soap operas. Earl Grey tea and gravy.'

Familiarity swims into your eyes. 'Where do I live?'

Here. Nestled in my heart and threaded through my bones, I think, *and always after I close my eyes, smudged behind that colourful, dancing blackness when our long days together have ended...*

I say, '72 Hill Cottage Road.'

'Hill Cottage?' You sound surprised. Delighted, even. You always wanted to live in a cottage; a thatched roof would be idyllic.

'But there's no hill, and it's not a cottage,' I hasten to add, for the third time this week.

'And... who are you?' you ask, wariness sneaking into your tone, your eyes not meeting mine, staring down and down, through your pale hands folded lightly on the blanket across your lap, your veins like overcooked spaghetti, liver spots sprinkled like a garnish.

I am yours, I think. *I am yours, and you are mine, and I do not want to do this—any of it—without you.*

'I am your neighbour,' I say, even though I am not.

'I am your neighbour,' I repeat, just to hear how it sounds.

Still Warm

K M Elkes

WINTER 2018 SECOND PLACE

The boy sits at the top of the stairs and waits for the smell to come. He is familiar with the kitchen scene below—a fat turd of ground meat smokes in a pan, his mother leans on the counter, the edge whitening ridges into her palms. The high shriek of the extractor fan, extracting.

Across the landing, his father grimaces round a shaving brush, then dips his razor and draws it down his neck. The boy remembers the stubble noise on his father's collar when he used to kiss him goodnight. Alive and mysterious, like radio static. His father looks at the boy, then double taps his razor on the sink and toes the bathroom door shut.

The boy slides down three more stairs, settles and waits.

Recipe For A Boy's Lunch:
One slice of thin white bread, unbuttered.
Ground pork or sausage-meat, fried the colour of night.
A shake or two of ketchup.
One slice of thin white bread, unbuttered.

His father says that she cries and stares and lies in darkened bedrooms with a damp flannel over her brow because she is a woman of a certain age, weak with her nerves. That whatever they do, they are quiet. That they do not disturb. His father says none of this is the boy's fault. Except, the way he says it, it is.

The boy slides down three more, settles, waits. He idles against the pale ribs of the bannister until he is finally called into the kitchen. Smoke hangs low as early morning mist. He remembers, as he always does, to say thank you as the wrapped sandwich is handed to him. It has the weight of a human heart.

His mother wets her fingers and slicks down a rogue lock on the boy's head, then sighs and kisses a cheek and tells him to behave himself. She smells of burnt meat.

Five years hungry, that boy. Yet as he sets off for school, he takes the same care as always, the same love as always, when he

feeds a neighbour's bin with that wrapped and blackened heart,
inedible and still warm.

Heartwood

Johanna Robinson

WINTER 2018 THIRD PLACE

I sit on the porch. There aren't many quiet moments like this. In our little village, there aren't many errands to run. The wood beneath my feet is old, the only part of the original house that is left; there are charred shadows in patches, and the black edges of the boards are lined and creviced like ancient knuckles, or lips. This ancient wood is greyer than the rest of the house, its rings harder. It's ten years, now, since we rebuilt the house. I'd watched Henrik fell the trees in the nearby woods. I'd marked each of them with a gash of red paint. I knew exactly which one the soldier had pushed me up against, which section of bark had scratched the skin between my shoulder blades, and the place either side of the trunk where my fingernails had dug into it. But I'd needed more than this one tree to go. All the others that I'd counted, back and forth, over the soldier's shoulder that thudded against mine, until it was over—they had to come down too. Henrik sliced open the trunks, roots to neck. He stripped the bark, split them over and over into planks, trimmed and sanded them until I was happy. Now they clad our bedroom, their grain like frozen waves. Henrik sanded them so well that when I lie in bed in the dark and pull my fingers across their surface, they feel like skin.

In the clearing, there are saplings.

Mistakes Multiplied by 3.14159
Marissa Hoffmann

His daughters are marching in Parliament Square. Their banners say *Global Warming's Not Cool*. And all he's ever wanted was to give them the world.

In the peace of his studio the globe maker preserves the discerning man's world. He guides a craft knife along the edges of petal shaped segments of map, each one to be carefully positioned and gummed by fingers made nimble from plaiting long blonde braids. He's a time lord, pausing a priceless moment for his customers. He inks in their gods and their jackals and colourwashes the yesterday coastlines.

He imagines them sipping their single malt from crystal tumblers in private leathery libraries; the diplomat, the explorer, the tycoon and the prime minister, holding the world in their hands.

Men with manicured fingernails whirl past wars and sandy famines, then pause aghast at the delicate brushwork in the butterfly wings blamed for the chaos. They shake their heads at giant blue whales hiding beneath an ocean of plastic, and they keep turning,

        turning,

                turning,

                        plotting,

from Baffin Bay all the way down to Deception Island.

The globe maker's girls put their trust in human instinct, they cuddle him and tell him *don't be afraid*. But his work is the witness, he transcribes mankind's story first hand and tells them *it's no bedtime tale*. He outlines the jagged borders redrawn and the shifting rivers damned.

It's a heavy weight to bear on rounded shoulders and a truth that's always been his prime meridian. Precision is the axis of his efforts, for it's only a globe maker who'll tell you, mistakes are multiplied by pi.

So, he's not asking the earth, his wishes are simple, he's a father at his core. For a time when the world has turned more than his days, and for the love of curious daughters of daughters,

he etches a tiny warm message on what's left of the Shackleton
ice shelf:

Keep this precious globe turning.

Hewn

Amanda McLeod

I am of rock.

I am sedimentary. The years settle and each leaves its mark, one on top of the other; a pattern of fine lines around my eyes, across my forehead. Pressed between the layers he finds tiny fossils. Tattoos, scars, broken bones. I tell him nothing, this geologist of me. Let him study what he finds. He is careful. My sedimentary skin crumbles easily. Like limestone, anything caustic will burn it away; but it also tells of rich life, long gone, that thrived around me.

I am igneous. My boiling core contained within, erupting without warning. The lava of my passion has cooled, hard and black and shining, obsidian. Deeper, trapped in the frozen magma of emotion, tiny light crystals of happiness would sparkle if they were polished. Granite builds a wall around me; impenetrable but for the occasional crack which once made me permeable. The geologist examines these cracks with gentle hands, lest he trigger an explosion.

I am metamorphic. The relentless heat and pressure of existence have compressed me into something new. Ribbons of colour streak through my chest, wave patterns that trace the shifts as life pushes in from everywhere. Sheets of cold marble, white rippled with impurities; once my soft skin, now harder and less likely to shatter. The stuff of art and temples, beautiful in skilled artisan hands.

My heart, long still and cold, was once carbon. It too is metamorphic; endless years have transformed it from a blackened lump. Shape and polish will reveal it as a flawless diamond. It waits, within my rock of self, for patience and a discerning eye to dig it out. My geologist surveys me with his fingertips. Tender words are his markers, as he records aloud his findings. He is slow and thorough.

Sideswipe
David Rhymes

On a short row of city shops, between the Oddbins and the Peking Garden takeaway, a bullet skims through his insides and plinks into a waste bin. A second prangs the metal brake of his blue BMX, just missing his hand but ricocheting upwards through his throat. A third zips past his knees, jams at an angle in the brick-work. The boy hears all three shots, distinct as bells. At first, he thinks of something hot and fast and fierce, a wasp maybe, the impact of the first being not hard, but clean and needle-fine. The second feels like a dull cuff. It takes his breath. He sees the high-speed car sideswipe the kerb with a front wheel, observes the hubcap grazing loose and bobbling up towards him like a quoit. In the front seat of the jacked car, about the same age as himself, and tending in his hand the metal object that has fed the brittle air that triple *tock-tock-tock* of sound, he recognises his assailant, dipping down, through shrieking wheel-spin and a scowl of smoke into the car before the bouncing wheels vacate the kerb and speed away. But then he does not notice anything outside himself but feels his insides blooming, ink dropped into water coiling, new sensation spreading, and he knows there will be some unfolding as the bicycle collapses under him, the world tips out of kilter, leans at a crook slant, and he is out there at the edge of meaning, where everything is curved and dopplered, stillness gathering and holding, and only certain small things shifting, like the awning, though this detail he finds soothing, and the blurred voice asking, 'Can you hear me, hear me?' with its folding echo, re-coordinating, fading, and his mother there surprisingly, first there, then gone, then there, then gone, his good hand with the pinch point of a needle leading to a line of saline binding him like gravity to earth.

Bare Minerals
Katie Nickas

These days, my skull is harder than ever—a gazing ball filled with clear, lucid visions ensconced in a base of ivory that never forgets.

My body is a hermetic chamber, and my brain knows its private thoughts. In this intimate space, I hear the rake of sinew and tendon, the whisper of bone on bone.

We're all in this together, hello, hello.

It happens by orderly regression—by air sighing in and out of joints. Time is an irreconcilable difference that's slow and drastic, like plate tectonics.

My skin robs the spotlight, crowd-sourcing photons. It has arrived and come into itself as the separate organ shown on charts and diagrams—the ones with clear-cut shapes and lines.

At the beach beneath the pier, there is a peaceful hum of waves. Trucks roll up and down the sand blasting oldies. Fishermen nab steelhead trout. It is all part of a system—whirring zoetrope of arms, legs, fins, and valves.

Rocks crumble down the cliff side as a hawk spreads its wings and pushes off the escarpment, meeting the naked sky. I feel it happen inside—jagged feldspar monoliths scraping the peak of my spine—the sound of nails on chalkboard.

Between these reprises, I've learned the truth: my body is a landscape, and the mineral world has grown indifferent to it.

Contents Fragile
Frances Gapper

I used to take in parcels for my not-next-door neighbour, who lives diagonally across the cul-de-sac; I suppose she'd nominated me as her person things could be left with, to be collected whenever she felt so inclined. If I happened to be dusting a front windowsill, I'd see the delivery man knock on her door and wait, then make a beeline—funny it's called a beeline, since bees from what I've observed tend to meander—for my house. And I always hurried to answer their knock or ring. No trouble, I'd say cheerfully. But if asked to sign I'd scrawl a wiggle, not the neat signature I learned in primary school.

Sometimes I'd try to guess what the package contained, by shaking and sniffing. I doubted it was all personal stuff; maybe she runs a little business. Her car's electric blue and she parks up on the pavement, thinking only of her own convenience. But I never felt resentful, not even when she just took the parcel from me and turned away, while continuing to chat on her phone. You're welcome, I'd say. After discharging my depot duty, I could relax and watch telly.

One evening I had to tell her no, your mother's already collected it. Hang on a moment—she paused the phone—what? Oh, I said, now I come to think, she didn't actually say she was your mum. I just assumed. A grey-haired woman?

It couldn't have been, she said, my mother lives in Ipswich. I got very upset and kept apologising for the honest mistake I'd made. She backed off and said not to worry, she'd claim on her insurance.

I went upstairs and sat on the bed. Tucked behind my chest of drawers, the box looked meek and innocent. Seals unbroken. Contents fragile.

Log
Robert Mason

The man who lives opposite comes out into his garden. His shirt is un-ironed, and his trousers crumpled; stains are visible, even from my odd perspective. He hasn't bothered with outdoor shoes, and his braces dangle. Par for the course.

He stands for ages, shaking his head, as if unable to comprehend how the plants came to be there. You might think that he's pondering strategy, but I've never seen him with secateurs to hand. Yesterday he stood, mesmerised, for so long that his mug tilted, decanting tea on his slippers. Seemingly as flummoxed by it as he is by his jungle, he hurled the whole thing into the undergrowth and stomped indoors.

The plot *is* wild. Shrubs that must have been planted out in orderly fashion, long before I ended up here, are now intertwined. Some are ruthlessly dominant, others cowed. The range of greens, and of leaf size and shape, is extraordinary; blossom tends to fight a losing battle against foliage.

I, too, would be cowed by such profusion but from here it seems exotic. Even under Northern skies I half-expect banshee macaws to explode from the canopy, or a tapir to shuffle on to the un-mown, shrinking lawn, perhaps followed by its delightful offspring, all dapple and trust.

I would love that.

I doze.

Later, there's no sign of neighbour or wildlife, though the jungle looks as lush as ever. Maureen is here, fussing over blister-packs and ointments. She notices my eye-movement, purses her lips.

'Eighteen months since his wife died. You'd think he'd have sorted that mess by now. Made a start, at least. Someone should have a word.'

How I dislike the woman, with her tabard and airs and mind-numbing bulletins about the village I never got to know. I need her, though, and I'm in no position to complain. Trying to ignore her soliloquy I submit to the pummelling and wiping, to what she calls *maintenance*.

I drift, helpless as a floating log.

When I open my eyes, Maureen has gone. Relieved, I look outside—but spy only hideous order: manicured lawn, power-hosed concrete, regimented annuals, polychrome gnomes.

The bitch has moved my mirror.

Hidden in Translation
Stephanie Hutton

I learn the language of ovulation: basal body temperature glides and the slick stretchiness inside that whispers 'now'. I don't tell you of course but lean my head on your shoulder to inhale your strength. My signals separate sex from its purpose. I dress as an anti-mother: seductive, made only for adult needs.

In cafes, on trains, at the supermarket, I sneak glances at little heads and ache to the mewls of new humans. My version of pornography.

Alone, I smooth out a tiny velvet sleepsuit that I picked up from the sales—*for a friend* I rehearse. I lay the outfit onto my chest as I clutch its empty sleeve. My fingertips hum their way down the material. Next to me, the solid oak drawer holds little white sticks with one blue line that just might change to two if I wait long enough. Quiet division. Signs of life.

My body instructs me. It must be now, or thirty-three long, long days away. I warm my wrists with Chanel and hover in the doorway. You lean forward watching sport on a luminescent screen. I hope that your team wins.

All Kinds
Monica Dickson

Jessica knows all the different kinds of rice; *Or-y-za sat-i-va, Or-y-za gla-ber-rima* she recites in perfect rhythm as she skips. She doesn't mention creamed, from a tin, and the other girl—the one with the fidget toy, watching from the wall—doesn't mention last night's tea was frozen peas. She sucked the sweetness from each one, every so often flicking one across the kitchen table towards her baby brother.

There's a bench at dinner break where you sit and wait for them to shout seconds. That's where the other girl, Bethany, eats her free school meal. This should mean she's first in the queue, but she doesn't take chances; she perches en pointe, the plastic tray bouncing off the fight-or-flight judder of her knees. When the call comes, there's no need to push or elbow, her weapons are persistence and a tooth-sharp charm. Once the stampede is over, Bethany hovers around a nearby table of children, watches them poking at their carefully curated packed lunches. She starts to strut, hands behind her back; an inspector. She sees the group folding inwards. Then she notices Jessica, who picks up a tiny pot of edamame and puts it down again. She doesn't look at Bethany, who leans in to comment on this yoghurt or that flapjack. Bethany prefers biscuits, but she'll take anything wrapped that'll fit in her pocket. If she touches their food they sometimes just leave it behind.

Bethany doesn't care about friends. Her mum's going to move her again anyway. The teachers are picking on her. And it's a long way to walk. Bethany walks on her own; she's got a phone if anything happens. When Jessica's dad, reverse parking on the yellow zigzags, nearly runs Bethany over, Bethany swears he did it on purpose. Her mum comes to school then and kicks an iron-shaped dent in his car's sliding door. She says Bethany can't go on residential either. She needs to look after her brother.

Back home, at the table, Bethany spins the pot of edamame on its unsteady axis. She'll travel when she's older, she reckons; *A-sia, Af-ri-ca, North-and-South-A-me-ri-ca* she chants, counting out the beans.

Loisach
Carlotta Eden

Go back to the rush of the river and trace your fingers over the wet wood of the bridge: the curve of your C, the tall lines of her V. Stand here, a grown woman with a career and kids and a husband ready to leave you. Go down to the water and roll the jeans around your knees. Feel fifteen again. Watch how the push is fast and fresh and green-blue like medicine. Remember the mermaid bruises on your legs, the *shuck-shuck* of the waves against your shins, the way your cheeks blushed blood as you ran into the water and how you held your breath as she lifted her arms above her head. Remember the sting on your skin after she slid the razor up to your thighs that morning, the red bumps left over for days after. Hold yourself steady against the current, wondering how far you'll go in, what you'll remember. Ignore the shake in your body as the water breaks against you. Look for those girls, taking off their dresses, their underwear, leaving their heels on the banks. Think of your kids safe in their beds, your husband's shadow lingering at the door. Stay here as long as you can. Watch the sun sink back behind the mountains, the cold fall into your bones. When you picture her face, tilted back against the sky, the damp ends of her hair like seaweed, listen to your heartbeat slow and steady, how it feels to be alive.

What We Talk About When We Talk About Lettuce
Tim Craig

Things had become so bad in our relationship that Kara and I were now communicating solely by means of a language based on the vegetables in our fridge.

For example, a head of purple-sprouting broccoli left on the worktop translated as, 'Has the dog been fed?' A bunch of six or more carrots was code for, 'Someone rang for you but didn't leave a message.' And a single bulb of fennel placed on the chopping board meant, 'Go fuck yourself.'

How our marriage had become quite so dysfunctional would take more than the entire fresh veg section of Morrisons to explain, but the fact was we couldn't afford it to go on like this much longer, if only because of Kara's insistence on buying organic.

Eventually, we decided to seek professional help. The counsellor we saw was very understanding, both of our problems and of the sack-loads of muddy produce we tipped out twice a week on the carpet of her consulting room.

She said that, while she had never encountered our specific issues before, she had, in fact, once helped a couple from Barnsley who communicated only by the medium of sea fish. I joked that we should probably get together with them, as I felt our own diet was somewhat lacking in protein these days, but neither Kara nor the counsellor laughed.

Although we attended the sessions for several months, at significant expense, it became increasingly clear that our differences were irreconcilable, and one morning, I found Kara sitting at the breakfast table in tears. She told me she just couldn't take it anymore. I watched her crying for a minute or two. I wished one of us had the courage to say what needed to be said. But I knew without even looking in the fridge that we just didn't have the words.

Imperfect Continuous

Perry Zyan

Numb white moonlight had long since unpeopled the street. Up high, behind double-glaze, the bone chill in Florent's fingers and feet ached mournfully despite the heating. Seventy years had dwindled into this recurring, solemn insomnia.

Florent had always believed in living life awake, in being a leader. To dominate was to invigorate, to incite, to know he'd be remembered. Strength was in his nature, he reminded himself, for cold was only the temporary absence of warmth. Endurance was the way. Belief.

Across, down there, and out, beyond the road with its tame pavement and its bus shelter, grew an unruly scrubland of branches. The whole lot had been cut back seasons before; he recalled the activity of contractors, refitting the streetlights one by one, replacing imperfect pumpkin orange with sleek, greyish downlight.

No one ever returned to tend the branches. With time, they had reclaimed their former growth, invading the light, splintering it into giddy patterns onto the ground below.

Cloud like a silken coat came in. Fast gaps of stars diminished, then faded to nothing.

Faraway gusts of breath sounded from the bed. In his life, Florent had never known a more comfortable chair than the one he now occupied.

Dutifully, he reached to the table and shook a pill from its lidless, plastic jar. Palmed, it became a moon without an orbit. With a movement like a slap to the mouth, he swallowed it dry. Minutes brought morning closer. Sleep came, pleasant as the taste of toffee.

Television was on in the room when he woke. Day—he blinked outside to where a shove of cars was stilling, delayed by something out of sight. Bus stop faces waited, stern with purpose, inside scarves and coats and silent steam-whistle exhalations.

She was awake as well, bustling, impatient for the illusion of hurry. Sustenance came, and routine, warm water washing age-loosened skin. Each day together was a pinnacle of days; like all others, it took away and gave back.

Florent turned from the window: as well not to feel alone; besides, what was left, but each other and the wintry certainty of acceptance?

Tide Pools
Katie Camlin

The place we meet is an empty beach. The water is a dark, murky blue and leaves tangled brambles of brown seaweed discarded on the shoreline. A curtain of fog blurs the edges of the water and the grey sky together, obscuring the curved coastline. A cool mist leaves saltwater kisses on my cheeks and nose and brings goose-bumps to the backs of my arms.

Tide pools dot the shore like freckles, each their own perfect microcosm; an entire ecosystem brimming with life. Sea stars float lazily amongst tightly clustered barnacles while hermit crabs scuttle precariously along the edges of their known universe. These creatures know nothing of the outside world, but we do.

We are always brought to this same empty beach. We always hold each other for a moment, standing where the sea meets the sand. The surf swirls around our shoes and our bodies pull together, desperate for our molecules to mix like the sand beneath us; we never know how long we'll have.

There's a small cottage tucked back a ways from the shore. It's old and worn; the sun-bleached walls are smoothed from years of battering by salt and wind, and white paint peels from the wooden frame.

No matter how many times we are brought back, it's always the same. The faint smell of cedar, a pile of broken logs in the faded brick fireplace, smoldering like they'd been abandoned only minutes ago. There is a couch the same deep blue as the waves, where we lie together beneath soft, hand-woven blankets, letting time spin away without us; its earthly rules don't apply here.

Within the cottage walls, hours and days unravel while the real world stands still. We lie there, lost in each other, electrified, not speaking; our bodies utter the truths that our lips are afraid to let escape.

We pull at each other, desperately hoping that maybe, this time, this will be permanent. That we can stay here, in this world without time, until our bodies fuse together the way our hearts have. That we can dive into a tide pool and live blissfully, know-ing nothing else but one another.

She Sleeps with Her Eyes Open
Shannon Savvas

She sleeps with her eyes open but never tells what she fears.

Perhaps, she says, I just want to avoid my nightmares.

At night, she lies, an effigy in their bed, barely breathing at the crunch of gravel on the driveway, holding the silence in her wide-open eyes. At the clatter of the toppled rubbish bin, she jerks then blesses the scavenger before curling like a pea-bug.

Sleepless, she prowls the house, lights out, peering through curtains, counting shadows.

Perhaps, she says, I'm not expecting anyone, just making sure the world is still.

Mornings, she puts on her face, eyes the fantail tapping at the bathroom window. A Harbinger of Death, Jack told her. Māori superstition.

Perhaps I am not ready yet, little Piwakawaka. 'Haere tū atu, hoki tū mai,' she tells the bird.

At work, she laughs, she works, and lunches with her girlfriends, drinking too many wines before returning to work.

Perhaps, she says, I could be this person.

But each time she changes her phone number, she knows it is only make-believe, like baby wishes for puppies, for wings, for a daddy who tickled her. She deletes his texts unread.

Fridays, she orders online Merlot, ice cream, chocolate to counterpunch salad bags, salmon fillets and frozen veggies. Her delivery slot—the hour after she gets home, before the street empties, before the dark rolls in.

Perhaps, she says, I'll never leave the house again.

Crammed into the rush-hour bus, she gags at the smell of sweat filling the spaces, when stray hands stroke her thighs, and anonymous hard-ons rub against her, thrusting between her legs.

Weekends curled in a corner, on the floor, she waits. The milkman rings. Her neighbour rat-a-tat-tats. The postman delivers more scrawled red apologies, like fire, like blood. They cram her letterbox.

Perhaps, she says, I'm waiting for someone to come and fill my hollows, someone to close my eyes.

Until one night, she can wait no longer. No one is coming. She lines up stockpiled bottles, empties stockpiled pill packets and opens the window to wait for the return of the Piwakawaka.

Perhaps the world is sweeter on the wing.

Hand Cream
Kezi Victoria

My mother has beautiful hands. She sometimes lets me rub cream into them, but not very often. She rolls her eyes and makes a phlegmy noise in her throat when I ask her. She laughs when I lay a towel on her lap and take her hand in mine. 'Beautiful, beautiful hands.' I sing. 'Strange child.' she says and casts an embarrassed eye at my father who doesn't look up from his book.

She purses her lips when I unscrew the lid, but I don't mind. I start with the thumb of her left hand; my mother is left-handed. I move in gentle circular motions from the wrist. She smiles at me, but her eyes look sad, and she has to swallow. She glances again at my father who licks his finger and turns a page. I massage her palm, tracing her life line looking for the part where I come in. Softly I stretch each finger and thumb. She sighs, and I wonder how long she's been holding her breath. She closes her eyes and makes a little noise in her throat, like mmm.

When I'm done, I kiss her knuckles. 'Happy now?' she says. 'Happy now.' I say. She pushes the towel from her lap and, straightening her skirt, rises to leave. She shyly pauses in front of the mirror to tuck her hair behind her ear. My father clears his throat and asks her what's for dinner.

Have We Got a Story for You?
Al Kratz

Stuck inside the beach house, hiding from a relentless rain, we are amused by houseflies the size of hummingbirds. There's no such thing as vacation—we are always working on something. We furiously write notes between telling stories about thunder and lightning. Nothing beats *that one time*. Remember when we saw lightning balls inside the house? Yes, in the dead center of the room. Electricity was in the air. Remember when lightning struck that girl at the ball fields? Yes, the streak of gray hair left behind. Luck was in the air too. We always believe we can find story. It's the way our eyes work, ready to receive. Our ears tuned to each other's voices. But sometimes thoughts get away from us before we can pin them down, and we hold funerals for the loss even if we don't always believe in the resurrection. We prefer life. We accept the weird with a twinkle in our eyes that says to each other do you see what I see? It's so special to face the strange. So easy to discard the boring. Why should the dull get light? We shove notes into our back pockets and judge the end of the storm. We think we're well-tuned, but we also know our imperfections. One of us will have quietly named a bird-sized fly Notorious. They will have given that fly an entire arc while the other unknowingly swats him down with an old rolled-up newspaper, opens the door, flings his body to the wind. One of us will be upset the other has murdered Notorious. We won't speak for hours. No one can say a word until our silence becomes the story.

Future, Tense
K M Elkes

You will sashay down the road, in your best white clothes and your golden streaks, spot-lit under street lights. You will MC yourself to the sky: 'I'm a Catherine wheel, a roman candle, I'm cherry bombs and firecrackers and skyrockets—I am the whole glittering display.' You will look back and ask me how very, how utterly *magnificent* I feel. You will use that exact word, 'magnificent'.

'Tell me,' you will say. 'Fill me up!'

In the absence of my words, you will shimmy close, traverse the circumference of my ear with your tongue, make it electric to the sound of your words.

There will be a thunderstorm near the horizon. In my head will be the first tease of it, static, a weight of heavy air.

You will dance on. You will spin and glide into the middle of the road. You will run, arms out, like an airplane ready to rise. You will tell the dark: 'I'm as tall as the night. A long drink of good wine. I'm a rose, a whole bunch of them, and the shovel and the fork. I'm the earth they grew in. I'm a Soil Jesus!' You will spin, and you will keep on spinning until you have spun perfectly. Then you will run over to me, idle on the pavement. 'Just try,' you will say, 'I want you inside out. Don't let me down now, I'm desperate!'

Only then will I speak. Make quiet words. Tell the truth. Try, this time. 'I want to be all the light, but I'm just flickering. I'm a tree root trying to break through a road, I'm a shivering dog. I'm alone on a platform watching the last train home. I'm a swing of the arms and a bunched fist. I'm the taste of blood and tight skin tightening. I'm the wearing of that scar.'

Above us, black leaves we cannot see will begin to stir. There will be a taste of dust in the air. 'Did you speak?' you will say and cock your head like a dog.

I won't reply. I won't feel it when the rain starts in.

Missing Person
Nicola Ashbrook

The Zanussi sheet always goes on the bottom—advert to ground—that's the rule. I carefully unfold Argos, taking care not to rip its fraying folds and place it reverentially on top. My mattress. I squat at the foot end, beside the wall, to check the corners. I move in a practised clockwise arc, pausing at each one to ensure a ninety-degree angle. I tweak and tease until I'm sure it's square.

Pillow next. I feel for each zip in turn, tugging them taut, ensuring the final tooth is gripped. I bump my fingers over the cobbled plastic to be certain. I place my pillow, openings downwards, exactly two-thirds of the way across the mattress, making sure there is a fraction of a gap with the wall: shiny orbs of condensation will be clinging there by morning.

I sit dead centre, using my forearm to measure the gap on each side. Just a centimetre to the left. I lie slowly back to test my position. My head only skims the pillow, so I wiggle backwards, flagellating myself for such poor estimating. Assured I am in the right place, I carefully hinge at the hips, buttocks grounded, up to sitting. I pull his hoody over my clothes. I smell his musk, but mercifully the unravelling doesn't come tonight.

I unwrap my 'eiderdown'—I sleep better calling it that—and arrange it the way Mary showed me. 'Always put the plastic on top,' she'd said, 'keeps you drier if they piss on you.' I tuck the end firmly under my feet, smooth the creases from the filmy black.

I angle backwards again until I'm in position and everything is where it should be. I hope for sleep.

My poster looks down on me questioningly. They're everywhere in this city: adorning every bus stop, tied to lampposts, plastered on billboards. But this one is my favourite because they've hung it straight.

'I'm here,' I tell it.

I'm not hiding, yet no one sees me.

I'm invisible now.

How to Value a Painting
Dave Murray

James believed in balance. For eight years, the six paintings on the dining room wall charted their relationship. His four to her two, a reflection of the ratio of their salaries (excluding bonus). Two years ago, he had grudgingly accepted equality, a muted print of the coastal town where they met. But James had never considered that Laura might earn more than him. Now four of the six frames in the dining room were hers, *a celebration* she had said as she replaced his reproduction French landscape with an original abstract portrait in blue. He hated it immediately.

'Feminine shapes, masculine colours, like it,' nodded one guest in approval. Each time they replaced a painting, for whatever reason, they threw a dinner party. Laura had decided two months ago that she was now a vegetarian, because of the planet, whatever that meant.

James knew that Laura had paid a month's salary. From the canvas, the perfect circles of two assured eyes fixed him throughout the dinner. The sweet potato stuck in his throat. He lifted his glass of red in front of his eyes, willing the wine to smear the painting. Silently he mouthed the new rule he would propose later in bed. Three paintings each. Forever. Because jobs nowadays aren't as secure as they used to be, are they?

It was important to find a balance. Surely they both knew that.

The Day We Met the Unicorn
Gaynor Jones

The doors open to reveal a ceiling draped with ribbons and stars. The children line up to give their token to the suspiciously large fairy and receive a pair of wings in return. You breathe it in. The hay, the glitter, the excitement. It's the kind of moment you've dreamed about since the scan showed you were having a girl.

As the music starts, you waddle over to a bale. The hay scratches your swollen ankles, and you try not to think of needles piercing your skin.

The children sing, filling the barn with their sweet voices. You tap on your belly and feel the bubbling inside you. You look around and wonder, *which one could you have been?* The one with the wide eyes and solemn expression? The cheeky one, inching towards the stage? The small one, clinging to her mother, excited but unsure?

The barn falls silent as the main doors open, then a wave of gasps as the unicorn is guided in. You can't help but laugh. The poor horse has been trussed up with stars threaded through its tail, a glittering horn strapped somehow to its head. You should feel sad, but it's too wonderful.

You pose for a picture and ask the fairy to blow some glitter across your stomach so that you can make a wish.

Maybe when your daughter is born, the crooked lines and dark spaces on the screen, the ones that lead to the words *incompatible with life* spooling out of your doctor's mouth, will in fact, turn out to be the tiniest of wings. Maybe you won't have to labour at all, maybe you will open your legs and she will fly out from beneath you, dusting the room in pink and purple stardust. Maybe she will unfurl her wings and fly over to your breast and loosen her tiny pink tongue to wrap around you. Maybe.

You take your souvenir picture and file it, and the memory, away with all the others you've made in the last few months, on the advice of the hospital counsellor.

Picnic at the beach.

First train ride.

The day we met the unicorn.

The Quiet Couple Next Door
Karen Jones

The next-door neighbours blew away in last week's storm. They hadn't been in Edinburgh long. About a year, I think. Refugee couple from—oh, now—I want to say Africa. Probably was Africa. We never spoke to them. I don't think anyone talked to them. Couldn't have understood them if we'd tried, though, eh?

They were weird. No matter what the weather, they were happed up in jumpers, scarves and coats. Always looked shivery and snottery and never smiled much after they settled in. Maybe they couldn't afford the heating. Never thought about that. But at least they kept themselves to themselves and didn't bother anybody, eh?

According to the news, they're still blowing around in the sky. Spotting them has become a national pastime. They were last seen hovering over Cornwall, holding hands. Reports say they looked happy.

Us and some of the other neighbours—the proper local ones—got to be on the telly. We said we'd welcomed them to our street, that they were our friends and we're pleased for them, but we miss them. The reporter got us all to shout, 'Come home soon, Zain and Sara!' At least we'd found out their names, thanks to all the coverage.

Now we're hoping the wind doesn't change direction.

Forgetting How to Breathe in Koh Samui
Amy J Kirkwood

The birthday cake was bright artificial white, the colour of strip lighting in a shopping centre. Icing leaked over the princess-pink plate's edges, dripping onto the table like wax.

'I don't know why you brought it. It's not like Ash *knows*.' Lucas stalked the hospital bed where their daughter lay half-dead, circling it like prey.

'I didn't bring it.' Charlotte turned towards the window, staring out at the palm trees that swayed like a crowd, lighters up, moving to silent music. The chair she was sitting in was, she could tell, designed to be comfortable. This meant that it didn't seem to fit her body at all, no matter which way she shuffled or shifted. Shards of what felt like glass poked out of the stuffing into her back, needle-sharp.

Last night, she had gone to the beach. The stars had been covered by thick wet clouds, but she had watched the black waves flick and twist and slap against each other like children playing a clapping game. Without the starlight, it had been December-dark. She'd escaped alone this time—no Lucas—to remember what it felt like not to share air.

Between Ashley's bed and the window, there was a London-bus-red cord with a handle. The writing beside it was in Thai, but it was clearly designed to be pulled in case of emergency.

Charlotte turned back towards Lucas, watching as he spiralled, and wondered when she would have to use it.

A Long Soak
Kezi Victoria

I am in love with my hands after a long soak. My puckered fingers a premonition; an assurance that there is a last chapter in there somewhere, and I might, if I wish, grow old. I am in love with submersion; my blood thrumming, singing I'm still here. Then that gasp of air that tears the veil, screaming, pleading Not yet! The almost reflections in the bubbles. A realisation almost realised. I'll pull the plug, and by the time the water drains away, I'll know.

There.

All there is to do now is wait.

Last year, during the storm that left the dead seal outside my front door (omen), the tide receded so far from the beach that they discovered the remains of an ancient forest which had been hidden beneath the water for millennia. How funny is that? Imagine if this was the ocean and I was the secret. I wonder what those tiny people should think of my hair, as wild as a forest to them. And when, over time, the water is drawn away entirely revealing my sleeping body in its naked completion, laid bare and goose-fleshed, how will they feel? What will they do when all that was true is proved false, and all they dared not dream was possible appears, huge and unavoidable, before them?

I feel heavy now, my weightlessness lost and with it some of my certainty. Almost all the water is gone, and what is known is still unknown to me. What happens if the water runs out and I still don't know?

And now it's over. There is no calling it back. I feel skinned. Like a nerve. It seems I am that forest, after all. Can I always have been? And do I know now? What was told to me by my blood, my grasping lungs, those puckered fingers. Was I pleading my own case, unawares? The water is gone now, and it seems that the decision is still mine. Perhaps I will let the water run again. Just a little.

Hold my breath.

Count to forever.

Soles to the Sky
Nicholas Petty

You always wanted an appetite for danger, and now here I am, up to my neck in bouldered snow. Beside me, your upturned ski-boots, half buried, the buckles burst open, a sliver of sock just visible. Above us, the rumpled slopes. They slipped like sheets of broken glass.

We've been dragged to the path of a chairlift and the unearthly twangs of its straining cables. The passengers are shouting down to us in French. *Aidez*, I call back, and they swing on by, craning their necks to watch two foreign fools.

I've heard you should spit when you're buried in an avalanche, to figure out which way is up. I've heard that's a mountain myth because an avalanche is a pummelling blender of rocks and ice. Do you still exist above the ankles? Do I still exist below the neck?

The helicopter is small in the valley, flitting past the craggy peaks like a fly in a quarry. I imagine the pilot and the winchman: leathery professionals, last night's *genepi* still on their breath. They will arrive too late. It is already too late.

Do you remember when we met in the hotel pool all those summers ago? When our parents went golfing, you performed for me. A flat-bellied dive, a gangly cannonball, then a handstand in the shallows, your legs nowhere near straight. I was impressed, not by your skill, but by your industry.

But you kept on performing. A calf amongst bulls in the rugby scrum. Off with the frontrunners until your legs jellied. Weeping home from meetings with hard-nosed men of business.

Your face was a picture when the snow cracked. A confession. But your legs are straight now. Soles to the sky. The best handstand you ever did.

Locked

H R Owen

'Just get rid of them,' he reasons. Always so reasonable. 'They don't go anywhere.'

'It's so I don't lose them,' I say.

'I only have two, I never lose them,' he says, misunderstanding.

Of the fistful, I use two every day—front door and bike lock. The others offend his logic. One is for a house my dream-self still calls home. Wrapped in sleep, I revert, and the stairs beneath my feet chant their rosary of creaks in heart-timed rhythm. Two more have held nothing of me or mine behind them for years, but there was a time when I lived behind them so bright and broad that light came spilling from the cracks around their edges. One, my right to use waxes and wanes with the tides of relationship, and I am never sure when facing its lock whether I'm supposed to knock or not. Another is a fake, a pun, a literal USB key, its files long corrupted but lingering in my memory with the taste of bruised fruit and cheap beer.

He's right, they are keys to nowhere, but not to nothing.

Dog Training for Cancer Companions
Jo Withers

Sit—Longer than is comfortable on hard, resistant hospital chairs. Like they were designed to increase anxiety. Scrutinize every public information poster without taking in a single word. Do not speak or try to lighten the mood. Appointments over-run and days disappear, but outside, life is fading anyway.

Fetch—Around the clock. You are now an emergency nurse with no training. You work the day and night shift. You jump every time he breathes deeply and bring water before he asks.

Play dead—Forget who you once were and every small thing which seemed important. There are no irritating days at work, no frustrations with the children, no sickness or worries for you. These are instantly dwarfed by his condition and would be selfish to mention.

Heel—Stand close-knit together, form a protective inner circle of privacy. Be mindful not to bore friends with suffering and setbacks. Keep situation contained. (Note: Sudden and un-expected bouts of tenderness can sometimes arise from the in-timacy of these dark times, but on other days you'll both feel claustrophobic.)

Beg—Constantly of everything. Hope harder than you thought was possible. Pray for the first time in thirty years. Make silent, supernatural pacts with the universe—if I get through the crossing before the lights change, his tests will show improve-ment. If it stops raining before we get home, he won't need the operation. Never drop the baton of worry or stop thinking about him for a moment or you will lose the game.

Rollover—Accept his mood, the backlash, his bitter envy of your health. Absorb his frustration. Deflect the stinging blows from his savage tongue. Remember it is just the treatment talking (screaming); somewhere underneath he is still the same.

Stay—Although sometimes you don't want to. Terrified by each new symptom. Wishing for just one normal day. Hoping you both reach the other side.

In [No] Man's Land
Marissa Hoffmann

The hard plastic of the upturned crates cuts semicircles into the skin of Yasim and her mother Raheima as they try to sleep. When they dress they turn more folds into the fabric of their saris than they used to.

'Mama, Santara has to wait inside since her days came.'

'Not for long,' Raheima says. 'Santara's father makes the shelters for the new people. He boasts he'll be the first to catch his daughter the best husband.'

Yasim begins to wonder who will do her catching for her.

*

'You hungry enough yet, Raheima?' says the old woman who passes daily with a cigar hanging from her mouth.

*

'When your days come, Yasim, send me a message,' says Santara.

'I'll tell the water boy to tell you; *the monsoon has arrived*.'

*

Raheima buries her wet face into her daughter's warm flat chest and kisses her on the head, 'come straight back.'

*

In the stone building there's a bed like the ones the old men make at the roadside; blue crisscrossed ropes and bamboo, 3000 Taka. And two boys in western trousers with zippers. They each take a turn. The second boy laughs to his friend, 'I didn't have to wait too long brother.'

*

The old woman bites down on her cigar with her back teeth, and from a fold in her green sari she hands Yasim two fist-sized bags of rice. Smoke turns inside her mouth and rolls over the peeled-back pink of her bottom lip.

*

The rain is loud on the plastic sheet roof. The mud and human waste slosh and collect against the sand bags. Their old home was better. A proper bed, big enough for Papa too.

Yasim won't say that to her mother, and she won't send the childish message to Santara.

Council Estate Gothic
Barclay Rafferty

We mostly eat Maris Pipers from the farm, except on Fridays when Mum sends me to the chippy. She comes home from work at midday to wash her hair and always has time for a cuppa before conditioning it.

She plans her priestlike afternoons around cups of Earl Grey.

*

There's always something new to see on the estate. Today it's vestal snow, sealed tightly against the concrete. Yesterday I swear I saw a UFO, but nobody'll believe me when they ask about its shape, and I reply, 'Like a blimp, mate.'

Caroline's cheeks beam like broken traffic lights. It's nice to see her face without Snapchat filters. 'Would you like to walk back wiz me?' I go to speech therapy but still can't talk properly.

'When have I ever lied to you, Caz?'

Words fog as I ask for mushy peas.

All the time, Dad...'

The pub sentinel hides secrets of unknown lounges beneath his herringbone cap, roll-up limping from an uncorrected underbite. He wakes when he wants to, deep in the lungs of the estate. His biggest worry is the 1:25 at Goodwood, or so I think.

I turn left onto our street and look up to Caroline's window. Every light in the house goes out, except the smartphone beacon.

*

On a scratchy projector behind NHS glasses, Mum looks over at me, eyes like unwoven indigo. The house always feels sick when she's depressed. She stares at the radio like the group is playing just for her inside the speaker, all thimble synths and *yeah-ee-yeah-ee-yeah-ee, ee-yo.*

People on the estate never mention mental health.

The cold really gets to Mum; she keeps the heating on full. Dad hates it. I gulp lemonade and see her in rainbows through the bottom of the glass. She looks over again for help, diazepam-eyed. Then he grabs her from behind, makes her whole world dark.

Chips fly and I just stare at the red motorbike revving through the forest till the screen fades, pure and black.

*

Half an hour later, Mum teaches me how to waltz. She *one-two-threes* in Primark slippers and I box-step around dinner in Grandad's pyjama bottoms.

Addicted

Faye Brinsmead

The back of his neck smelt of barley. It was as creaturely as a small marsupial. Invisible down covered soft white skin. Somewhere beneath, a pepita-sized heart must be fluttering. The dark thatch of hair on the pillow was another loved animal. The two slept peacefully in air as cool and cloistered as well water. She lay awake, lulled by the fragrance, the concentric ripples.

These nocturnal things dug tiny sharp teeth into her heart. They reconciled her to his daytime selves.

On their first date, they roamed from pub to pub. At a pedestrian crossing, waiting for the lights to change, he came clean. He always did, she discovered later. It put the woman under an obligation. To help. To stay.

His breath hissed slightly when he spoke. His low-set jaw, like a ventriloquist dummy's, ate into his chin. Surely facial architecture wasn't destiny. He could change. He'd done it before. The bait was that he was trying again for her. The trap: any failure was hers.

She learnt certain facts. Alcohol stays in your system for seventy-two hours. As the poison leaves your liver, it fumes into your mouth. Anything enraged him. They argued in cars, and she found herself at home, alone. She could erase his messages but not muffle the cries of the nocturnal animals. A time-loop kept bringing her to his door, always around 8 p.m. He had hung a green satin dressing-gown over the glass pane so strangers couldn't snoop.

As soon as she was inside, she remembered how cramped it was, at the bottom of his well. He disliked going out, except on benders. Only Premier League soccer and *South Park* were worth watching. He worshipped Liverpool. On this side of the green dressing-gown, everything she thought she was shrivelled like an unwatered lawn. It crept away, knowing no one wanted to know. But she felt it pooling between the walls of her acquiescence.

When he accused her of hanging around until he married her, she left. Indignation caged the night animals for long enough to break the loop.

On sleepless nights the scent of barley nestles in the curve of her neck.

Summer Party (How It's Done)
Valerie Fox

Nonetheless, go to Kerm's. It's outdoors. You were invited. But don't go just because you are invited, or because there has been a ceasefire. Follow the marked-up map in your pocket and wear (in your mind, at least) your nana's mink coat.

Try to avoid intimacy. Avoid taking any perishables, like grapes or your soul. This will help when it comes time to escape.

Listen, nodding, as Scott delineates the plot of his new science fiction novel, over and over, on repeat. Notice Kerm's super self-aware dog has had enough and has gone inside to gaze out at you through a glass door.

Next house over, an animated, familiar sort of light shines through an upstairs window. The light pulses and disappears as quickly as it starts.

The overall party sound gets turned up just at the moment the light leaves, along with Linda's entrance. Linda is alone. It's conspicuous. There's a break, like a record skipping.

Now is time to go back inside yourself and think-draw pictures of well-known arcs and gestures. Or help some elderly rich people speaking Italian get off the train and wend their way upstairs and across the field-like distance to an awaiting car.

The full moon staggers from branch to branch. The time it takes for you to reply to a question is equal to the distance between the kids' swing-set and your listening place in the corner of this outside room. It's called a deck, we're on a ship.

Deaths and Accidental Entrances
Andrew Leach

There you are. Vital in an Eden of ripe, wanton lilies, their chloroform scent hard at work, your overnight bag reclining on the scarred parquet. The welts of nervous heels as remnants of past assignations. A stag looks down on the front desk, imperious in his gilded restraints, a seen-it-all-before smirk rendered in oils. We come together in an ephemeral embrace. Your perfume binds me in chains, and I'm Harry Houdini, filling my lungs as the tank bubbles. From somewhere I hear you say we should go through.

Seven of us occupy a dozen chairs leaving seats for ghosts, the last autumn leaves of a family tree ravaged by the storms of age, of drink. Our separation made less by the magnetic heft of aunts and the temptation to wilfully forget. The uncousining of distance. Here for formality yet impolite as the rain, squirming in shouldn'ts and mustn'ts. The clerk precise, the will sober as a parson, the bequests generous and impractical.

And afterwards, awash with tea and remembrance, standing stifled by worsted and silk, we exchange glances over china lips and delicately decline lifts and the ordering of taxis. Excuses are dredged from an ancestral well and hauled into plausibility, breathing the blind, trembling air. Later, we talk of committing futures to eggshells, treading softly so as not to wake the dead, save for those lonely moments when we writhe and dance.

Ain't No Cure for My Fibonacci Blues

Jupiter Jones

August.
Remember.
Aunt Myrtle's
Four weeks' holiday.
Five Siamese and old Finklepus.
Her cats in wicker baskets like lobster pots.
We went to the harbour for whiting; boiled fish, stinking the house out.
Fish crammed into jam-jars stacked in the refrigerator, enough for a week at the rate of one per cat per day.
On the way back from buying the fish we would stop at a beach, somewhere wild and windy and run through the dunes and get sand in our shoes and shells in our pockets.
Driving about in her old mini, you in the back and me in the front, perched on the side of my seat, my foot over in the driver's footwell to press the clutch because she had gout in her left big toe, so I clutched, and she shifted gear, shouting 'press, and hold, and release'.
Back to her clean house with Ercol chairs in pale wood, and diverting books, and risqué pictures, and a yoghurt-maker, and Nina and Frederick playing on the gramophone; sipping cider through a straw, and cats.
And everything was allowed, like cake for breakfast, and reading all night, and drinking cocktails, and dressing-up, and swearing; what larks!
Some days we visited castles, chased peacocks, swam in the lido, got lost.
Once we saw a cohort of Roman soldiers.
Marching grimly along the A6.
Heading back home.
Not them.
Fool.
Us.

My Coat
Jane Allen

I bought it in the Oxfam shop in 1998 for £12; an impulse buy. Dark grey, ankle length with turn up cuffs, a vent up the back and a striped lining, now in tatters. An overblown size eight with preposterous shoulder-pads, it was clearly made for the New Romantic '80s market. With the shoulder pads taken out, it is perfect with a cloche hat and button boots, good with jeans and classy over a suit with heels, leather gloves and a briefcase. However I wear it, whether I'm stout or thin, my shadow on the ground or reflection in a shop window is familiar: part dashing and part Tiggy Winkle. I have flirted with other far more expensive coats since, but in my wardrobe clearouts, those are the ones to go.

I have hugged it round me to smoke in the cold, rain and snow outside four addresses and dragged it off its hanger, racing to catch a rainbow, a sunset, a thunderstorm or shooting stars.

I have worn it to meetings and been glad of it as a blanket and a dressing gown in poky B&Bs; pulled it over my knees on bitter railway stations, waiting for the last train home.

It has flapped around me, coat-tails billowing, on the seafront in Whitby and Brighton; flipped round my ankles on icy pavements in London and tripped me up stairs and escalators everywhere.

It has been thrown on seats in waiting rooms, consulting rooms and on floors in friends' kitchens. I have sat for hours in it on plastic chairs under hospital lights in Leeds, Bradford and Harrogate, waiting for a bed, calming my mother's disordered impatience or watching her heart monitor as she slept; wondering if this would be the last time.

It brushed the knee of a man who was not my lover as I kissed him goodbye, chaste on the cheek; wrapped me as I walked upright away; stopped my heart from flying apart.

It comforts me as I sit and smoke and face my dying, maybe sooner but more likely later, as the crystal precipitation grows in my brain.

Do You Stop at Tavistock Square?
Gary Kaill

You confront the city as it wakes and quickens. Its people and vehicles carry the weight and the violence of an uprising. You fiddle in your jacket pocket for your phone because you think you feel it vibrate, but, on closer inspection, it has not, so you put it back.

Then.

You are lying on steps—stone steps, crumbling and cropped, their edges rounded and protruding—and you are arranged in a way that is troubling, and you decide to block out that which you may not wish to know.

But then there is blood, and that causes you to manage the approaching fear and upset—you will not scream or cry—in a measured way. The blood is on your legs, but your legs are merely heavily grazed. There is no blood elsewhere. The pain is in your left elbow. Jacket? You do not move at this moment because movement may reveal things that are worse. Broken things.

From the steps, your view of the street is wrong.

You lift your head.

There are things in view that you cannot process.

A bus. You focus on the bus. Its vast redness is a beacon of safety: look at this. Be distracted by this. But the bus begins to change shape. Very slowly, it folds in on itself, its tall sides peeling magically away from its chassis. As this happens, the large number thirty at its front pops away as if blown through by a hot, cruel wind.

You do not know if this is happening now or if it has already happened. Time, you realise, is just completely fucked.

Glass sprays, jubilant and magnificent and people respond, in time, with its glorious momentum. They are perfectly in time: a dance in which partners dare not miss a step. When the dance is over, the dancers lie down, buckling themselves to the throbbing ground, arranged imperfectly and afraid to let go.

You want to be like them, want to follow their movements which are beautiful and terrible.

Warm liquid slowly creeps down your left cheek. Everything goes quiet. Or does it?

Sirens.

You place your head on the ground.

Every Second Thursday
Elaine Mead

We'll wish for more but keep quiet about it. The silence will fill the air. Subtle at first, until it becomes too much and finally begins to take shape. It starts in the corners, half-formed and blurry, gathering like the dust mites under the bed that we only remember to vacuum once a month.

Then it starts to float around us, leaving little grey bubbles as it trails about the house. We make an effort to try and stem its alarming growth. I tug the words right out of my mouth and scrunch them into a ball. I throw them to you, hoping you'll catch them and pass them back, but they fall short, landing at your feet. You pretend not to notice. At one point I watch you collect the cotton wool silence from the air in front of you and place it in your ears. Blocking me out. Deliberate.

I give up when I catch you conferring with the elephant in the room. A direct insult to our previously unwritten contract not to acknowledge it. I pluck the silence from my sleeve, it's grown thick like lint, and flick it at you when I think you're not looking. I watch your neck grow red with the effort of containing your frustration.

The silence has taken on full form. It's slightly taller than me, with slimmer hips and bigger tits and longer hair. I come home from work early one day and find you whispering in its ear, your hand on what I suppose is a thigh.

I remember that time we walked on eggshells and the short reprieve it granted us. Their deceptive hardness immediately pliable underfoot. We welcomed the noisy crunch, the way it bellowed and shoved the slowly creeping silence out of the room.

You walked away afterward as I scrapped the mess into an old cardboard box. I left it out on the street for the bin men to collect.

They come every second Thursday.

Holes
Sally Bosson

We meet each week, Diane, Lorraine and I. Just for coffee and a chat. Sometimes cake if Diane has made it, but since she lost her finger in the gardening accident, she hasn't made *any*.

Sunlight filtered in through the curtains, giving life to the fizzing dust and the bright steam rising from our mugs.

We started the same way most weeks, chatting about our kids. Our grown-ups. My daughter sent photos of Australian beaches, Lorraine's son had joined the US Navy, and Diane's boys had just opened a coffee shop in town. I missed my Allie. Feeling the catch in my throat, I changed the subject.

'Something's wrong with my washing machine, everything comes out with these bloody holes,' I said, pointing at my blouse where a tiny tear in the fabric had just started. It was new from George at Asda.

'M-hm,' said Lorraine. 'I've seen that before. Watch you ain't got a bobby pin floatin' around in there.'

Lorraine's greyhound, Charlie, snoozed peacefully by our feet.

'Tell you what is full of holes,' she continued, in her Southern American drawl I could listen to all day. 'My damn backyard. This guy is a real digger.' We all looked out into the garden where mounds of brown earth speckled the lawn. Lorraine had adopted the hound when her husband had left her for his dentist last year.

Diane put her coffee on the edge of the piano and reached down to scratch Charlie's ear. 'Look at that face, I could never be angry at those eyes,' she cooed.

'You know, he howls somethin' awful when I play that piano, Di.'

Diane laughed and pulled out the stool. 'You're pretty bad though, Lorraine. Still, I *have* to hear this!'

She began to play. Honestly, Diane became beautiful when she played. But this time, there were strange gaps, little holes, in the music where there weren't before. Charlie stayed quiet.

When she'd finished, Diane sighed and held up her hand, the gap between her middle finger and thumb impossibly wide.

'It's gone, but I still feel it, you know?'

We nodded. We knew.

ALSO FROM REFLEX PRESS

CHLOE TURNER

Witches Sail in Eggshells

'Witches sail in eggshells,' I heard Meg say from behind me, and I looked back. She was pounding the shells, hard, with the palm of her hand on the flat of a knife.

Bewitched by 'the sort of girl who'd batter your heart like a thrush with a snail on a stone', a woman overlooks the one who really loves her.

A seaside community is overwhelmed when the sea begins to expel its life forms. But the villagers would rather raise the sea wall, whatever the cost, than confront their past mistakes.

A woman's beloved garden withers as the baby inside her flourishes. When the pregnancy reaches its end, the progeny is not as she expects.

A widower feels like his life might have been a quiet nothing, but he'll end it with the flight he's always dreamed of. Even that fails, but instead of indignity, in the attempt he finds peace.

Perceptive, intriguing, and beautifully told, Chloe Turner's debut collection explores the themes of love, loss, the little ways we let each other down, and how we can find each other again.

HEATHER MCQUILLAN

Where Oceans Meet

Where Oceans Meet is a collection of sixty-one flash fictions from award-winning New Zealand writer Heather McQuillan.

Though small, the stories in *Where Oceans Meet* are substantial, often moving, and impressive in their employment of detail. They bring to the page varied perspectives and diverse aesthetics from a realism to surrealism.

These are stories in which characters yearn for connection but sometimes find, as in the title story, that 'when the vectors of the oceans' wave fronts meet at an angle, sometimes they cancel each other, sometimes they compound with spectacular results'.

BARBARA LOVRIĆ

Some Days Are Better Than Ours

Some Days Are Better Than Ours: A Collection of Tragedies Big and Small is the debut flash fiction collection from County Kerry based author Barbara Lovrić.

These pieces are in turn brutal, bittersweet and bewildering, but all challenge. By steering away from euphemism, these stories get to the realist heart of the human experience.